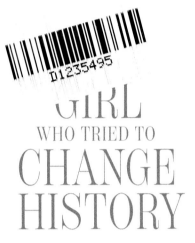

GIRL
WHO TRIED TO
CHANGE
HISTORY

Melissa Kaplan

THE
GIRL
WHO TRIED TO
CHANGE
HISTORY

a novel

MELISSA KAPLAN

BOLD
STORY
PRESS
WASHINGTON, DC

Copyright © 2023 by Melissa Kaplan

All rights reserved. No part of this book may be reproduced or used in any manner without written permission of the copyright owner except for the use of quotations in a book review. Requests for permission or further information should be submitted through info@boldstorypress.com.

This is a work of fiction. Apart from well-known historical events and locales that figure in the narrative, all characters are products of the author's imagination. Any resemblance to persons, either living or dead, is entirely coincidental.

First edition: June 2023
Library of Congress Control Number: 2022923537

ISBN: 978-1-954805-42-2 (paperback)
ISBN: 978-1-954805-43-9 (e-book)

Text and cover design by KP Design
Author photo by Jessica Somers

Printed in the United States of America
10   9   8   7   6   5   4   3   2   1

For my mother and my grandmothers

How could I have been so ignorant? . . . So stupid, so unseeing, so given over to carelessness. But without such ignorance, such carelessness, how could we live? If you knew what was going to happen, if you knew everything that was going to happen next—if you knew in advance the consequences of your own actions—you'd be doomed. You'd be as ruined as God. You'd be a stone. You'd never eat or drink or laugh or get out of bed in the morning. You'd never love anyone, ever again. You'd never dare to.

MARGARET ATWOOD *THE BLIND ASSASSIN*

I must study politics and war that my sons may have liberty to study mathematics and philosophy. My sons ought to study mathematics and philosophy . . . in order to give their children a right to study painting, poetry, music, architecture, statuary, tapestry, and porcelain.

JOHN ADAMS SECOND PRESIDENT OF THE UNITED STATES

What happened, after all, was only what had to happen. There were no dice in heaven.

HERMAN WOUK *THE WINDS OF WAR*

CONTENTS

PART THREE

PART ONE

Prologue

THE FUNERAL

October 15, 2009
London, England

I t was a dark, gray, gloomy London day—rain misting but not quite falling, no sun on the horizon. The cemetery ground that had softened slightly due to the recent rains was now dug up, ready to receive the body of another fallen hero. Ashes to ashes, dust to dust.

This body belonged—or had once belonged—to a man who had managed to achieve quite a lot before his inevitable return to the dust from which he had emerged nearly a century before. Although he had little in the way of family or close friends left by the time he died, having outlived nearly all of them, his service was nonetheless well attended due to his reputation. University professor, writer of history, drinker of black tea, lover of crossword puzzles—that was how most of the people present knew and remembered him. By the time he died, he had become almost the perfect symbol of an England long gone.

But perhaps his greatest achievement—though he himself might have disputed this—was noted in his obituary in one of the London papers, which several of the mourners clutched in their hands: "Group Captain Andrew Sheffield, RAF pilot, Second World War."

Before he was a university professor, scholar, and crossword enthusiast, he had been a fighter pilot, one of those who stood in the breach to defend his homeland from downfall seventy years earlier and lived to tell the tale. Many tales, in fact. In later years he would sometimes regale his students with stories about his flying days— usually after a few whiskeys—but he didn't do so very often. Bragging was not his style, nor did he ever consider himself a hero. He had simply done his duty, as he'd seen it, and been lucky enough to make it out alive. Not all his friends and loved ones had been so fortunate.

Professor Sheffield had been a fixture around Oxford University for several decades before retiring fifteen years ago, and many of his former students had turned out in the rain today to send him off on his final journey. Most of them knew little about his personal life, however, and were taken aback by one line in the obituary in particular:

"He is predeceased by his father, Randall Sheffield, his mother, Jane Dalton Sheffield, his brother, Anthony Sheffield, and his wife, Vivienne Sheffield."

"Wife?" many of the attendees asked in puzzlement, turning to one another. "I never met his wife, did you?"

"No, never. He never spoke of her either. Wonder how long ago she died?" For no one could ever remember any middle-aged woman in sensible English tweed joining Andrew at faculty receptions or Christmas parties. He had always been a bit of a recluse, his private life shrouded in secrecy. For all the accomplishments of his impressive long life noted in the obituary, the man himself had been an enigma to most of them.

Most, but not all. There was one person present on that cold, gray day who knew the full story.

Towards the back of the crowd of mourners was a young girl, probably in her late twenties, with blond hair and blue eyes. She was dressed in funereal black, and her bearing was solemn and restrained. She had tears in her eyes, but she did not let them fall. She was probably a former student or some distant relative—if asked, she would have claimed to be a grandniece. Yet she watched the casket being lowered into the ground with a strange intensity, and the heartbroken eyes of a young widow.

Few people at the service noticed her presence, which seemed to be how she wanted it. Before the minister had finished intoning his remarks, she left the cemetery, walking quickly and not looking back. "*Ashes to ashes, dust to dust.*" No need to stay longer once those words had been uttered.

Vivienne Sheffield had been through all this before.

1

THE PARK BENCH

April 12, 2009

B efore I begin to tell this story—to try to tease out the delicate strands of time and place, of action and reaction, of cause and effect, of joy and tragedy—I should begin by asking you a question: Do you believe in time travel?

I know. Of course, you don't. Neither did I, until April 12, 2009. That's the day this story begins, although I don't know if that's really an accurate way to describe it. What happened on that day changed my life forever, but to call it a "beginning" might be wrong. A circle has no beginning; there is no starting point to an endless loop. At least, that's my opinion. But I'll let you read my story and decide for yourself.

So, on to that fateful day.

April 12, 2009, was a day like any other. I wouldn't even remember the date except that what happened then set this strange chain of events in motion. Otherwise, it was completely unremarkable—except for me and the people whose lives would be altered irretrievably by what happened as a result.

I was sitting on a bench in a little park that I often visited, down the street from my apartment and not far from the university library. I was trying to finish my dissertation, which, if all went according to plan (ha!), would result in my finally, finally getting my PhD in history next month after seven years of graduate school. I was burned out by the effort, to be sure, but also driven. This had been my singular focus for years. It was the only thing I'd ever really wanted to accomplish, so I could do the only thing that I'd ever truly wanted to do: teach and write about history for the rest of my life.

I was typing away on my laptop, immersed in the political dramas and machinations of Western Europe in the late 1930s, when something made me look up. I noticed that an unfamiliar man had taken the seat next to me on the park bench.

The sight was not startling at all, and certainly didn't seem portentous. He looked like anyone, and like nobody. Another anonymous, middle-aged man, reading a newspaper, in no way doing anything that would attract my attention.

Until he spoke my name.

"Hello, Vivienne," he said, keeping his head down and his eyes on his paper.

My head snapped around to look at him again, more closely. I didn't recognize him at all, but he certainly seemed to know me. He was too old to be a fellow student, but maybe a professor, or someone else who worked at the university?

But he didn't look friendly. I don't mean he looked unfriendly, but it didn't seem like he had recognized me and was trying to begin a polite conversation. He kept looking down at his paper, yet it seemed clear he was waiting for me to answer him.

"How do you know my name? Who are you?"

"That's not important. As to how I know you—that will soon become clear. I need to speak with you."

"Umm . . . I'm a bit busy right now, actually." I generally don't make a habit of chatting with unfamiliar men sitting next to me on park benches. Who has the time or inclination for that?

"Clear your schedule. This is very important."

He finally looked up at me, and I could see him more clearly. My impression didn't really change on closer examination—an ordinary-looking man of fifty or so, light brown hair, brown mustache, glasses perched at the edge of his nose. His voice was slow and droning, yet something about it disturbed me in a way I couldn't explain.

I should have ignored him. But something told me that was not a viable option.

"Okay," I said finally, putting aside my laptop and turning to him with resignation, already trying to mentally calculate how long this would take and how much my writing schedule would be thrown off today as a result.

"So, Vivienne," he remarked, "we meet at last."

"At last? What do you mean?"

"I've been trying to arrange a meeting with you for quite a while. You always seem to be surrounded by people, and I need to speak with you alone."

"Oh?" I forced myself to look straight into his eyes, trying to play it cool, as bewildering as this whole conversation already felt. I didn't know the half of it yet.

"Right. I'm here to talk to you about your assignment."

"Um . . . my assignment?" The only assignment I currently had was the dissertation draft sitting on my laptop that I was supposed to be working on. I couldn't imagine what he was referring to. "What—ah, what assignment do you mean?"

He looked directly at me and spoke the last words I'd ever expected to hear, "Your assignment to help change history."

2

THE EXPERIMENT

I stared at him. He looked perfectly normal—boring, in fact—but I knew I'd heard him correctly, which meant he was obviously insane.

"I have no idea what you're talking about."

"Of course, you don't. That's why I arranged our meeting today—to explain it all. Please," he said, gesturing me back to my seat as he saw me begin to rise.

I considered making a run for it. There was no rational reason for me to stay and listen to this clearly disturbed individual, and yet something about him compelled me to sit back down.

"Okay. You have two minutes to say something that makes sense to me, or I'm leaving." I tried to look braver than I felt in issuing this challenge, but I don't think I fooled him at all. He simply looked amused.

"Oh, this will take longer than two minutes, Vivienne. But you are correct, time is of the essence. But then it always is. You, a historian, should appreciate its value more than most."

"How do you know I'm a historian? How do you know who I am, period?"

He brushed aside the question with a flick of his hand. "That's not important. Let me explain to you why we are here today. You will be pleased to know you've been selected for our program."

"Program? You mean, like a fellowship?" I'd applied for several academic fellowship opportunities to do post-doc work in case the brutal race for an entry-level teaching job in academia didn't pan out.

"You could call it that. But it will take place outside of the classroom."

"What do you—"

"Please, no questions for a moment. There is much to tell, and I want to get through it before you begin peppering me with your incessant queries. Let us go back to your apartment to discuss this in private."

I nearly laughed, then thought better of it. "Um, excuse me, but I don't know you at all. I'd rather not have any kind of discussion in my apartment if you don't mind."

"I can understand that, but this is a sensitive matter that should not be discussed in the open, and time is of the essence. I promise you, if you find what I tell you too upsetting or unpleasant, you can ask me to leave, and that will be that."

I regarded him warily. I was annoyed, but at this point, I was also intensely curious about who this man was and what he could possibly want from me. And judging by his slight size, I figured my skills from kickboxing class would allow me to dropkick him fairly easily if he turned out to be a dangerous lunatic.

I nodded my agreement to proceed and gestured for him to rise and follow me. We both walked the two blocks to my apartment in silence, and I let him in and offered him a seat on my second-hand sofa before nodding tersely for him to continue.

"All right. Let us begin."

I don't think I could recount everything that strange man told me over the course of the next hour if I tried. For one thing, once he began delivering his message in earnest, and I learned what it entailed, I'm pretty sure I was in shock. What he said made no sense, yet he conveyed it in a manner that left little room in my mind for doubt. Perhaps that was why he had been selected for his role of outreach: he had a way of convincing people of the impossible.

I'll just share the most essential parts of what he told me, as simply as I can. I learned more later, of course, but this was my introduction to what I would come to call "The Experiment," an experiment that would alter my life forever, though its intent was to alter far more than that.

"My name is Gunther. I am an ambassador, and I will be your contact from here on out. You have been selected on the basis of various qualities you possess for participation in an Experiment that involves, at its most basic level, time travel...."

"Wait—what did you say?" I couldn't help interrupting here. I mean, really ... time travel?

He seemed not to be surprised by my interruption. I imagine he'd had this conversation many times before, and probably few people could let that phrase pass without question. At least, I would hope not.

"Correct. But time travel is only a tool. The Experiment is a much larger undertaking."

He paused, looking at me to gauge my reaction, probably trying to see if I was still listening or on the verge of throwing him out. Both seemed like viable options to me at this point, but for the moment, I remained in my chair. Even if this man was utterly crazy—and disturbingly, I had a strong sense that he was as sane as I was, for whatever that might be worth—I still had to hear the end of this story.

Seeing I was not about throw him out, he began speaking again, in the same monotone voice, telling me the most extraordinary tale I had ever heard.

"In 1945—as you, a historian of the Second World War, will, of course, be well aware—the United States dropped the most fearsomely powerful weapon in history, the atomic bomb, on Hiroshima and Nagasaki. Shortly thereafter, Japan surrendered, and the war was over. The human cost of the conflict was enormous: tens of millions killed, trillions of dollars expended, land and property destroyed that would take decades to rebuild at great cost.

"The US government had spent years painstakingly assembling a coalition of scientific geniuses to create a weapon that would end the war. Now their work was done. But the question was raised: What to do with all the brilliance that had been channeled into the atomic bomb project? Would the participants all go their separate ways and never work together again? Or was it possible to channel the infrastructure that had been created over the past several years into an even bigger undertaking?

"A weapon had been created to end the war, and it had—though it cast a shadow over mankind's future existence on this planet. This got some people to thinking: Wouldn't it be even better if science could come up with a way to ensure that the war never happened in the first place?

"The idea was floated in utmost secrecy. Some of the scientists who had worked at Los Alamos on the atomic bomb project stayed on; others were recruited who had specialized knowledge of the type of work that would need to be done. For the next three decades, they toiled at their task. In 1976, the breakthrough came: time travel at last became a reality."

"Wait—wait just a minute. You're telling me that, for thirty years, there was a massive secret US government project trying to make time travel happen?"

He nodded. "Precisely. And it succeeded, as I said, in 1976. Since then, bit by bit, the Experiment has progressed."

"And what is the "Experiment?"

He looked steadily into my eyes for a moment, as though weighing his next words.

"The Experiment, Vivienne, is an ongoing project to change the history of the twentieth century."

3

THE ASSIGNMENT

I sat there for a moment, too stunned to form a coherent thought. Then I spoke, feeling certain of the truth of my words. "You're insane."

"I assure you I am not. I realize that what I'm telling you is shocking, and you may need some time to absorb it all fully. But as I said before, time is always of the essence in my work, so please allow me to continue without further interruptions for a bit longer. Then we can discuss next steps."

I shook my head, not to signal no, but in disbelief. None of this made sense. But I had a strong feeling that nothing would stop Gunther, crazy or not, from telling me the rest of his tale, and I wasn't sure my feet would support me if I tried to stand up and order him to leave now anyway. So, I kept sitting there, and he took that as an affirmation that it was okay to continue.

"As I explained, our goal is simple. We are endeavoring to change the history of the twentieth century by finding a way to eliminate its greatest disaster: the Second World War. To do so, we are using the relatively new discovery of time travel. We've found a way to send people back to various points in time, before and during the war, to try to . . . effect changes."

My head was still spinning. "I'm sorry, but this is insane. You can't change history after the fact—I mean, you can reinterpret it in new ways, obviously, but that's completely different. You can't actually change what's happened in terms of the facts. It's dangerous even to con-template that."

"Well, we're doing more than contemplating it, Vivi-enne. We're actually doing it, as I speak. And we'd like for you to join us."

"What?" I couldn't contain my gasp. What the hell was this man suggesting now?

He looked at me solemnly across the table, almost as if trying to decide if I was a worthy recipient of his next request.

"Let me explain this in a bit more detail. You don't need to know everything now, but I can begin to share a picture with you of what we're doing, so you can understand the implications and what your role would be—if you choose to accept it."

"If I choose? So, I have a choice?"

"Of course, you have a choice." He snorted with deri-sion at my simplicity. "You're not a slave; we don't have the power to force you to do anything you don't want to do. If you join the Experiment, it will be of your own free will—and with full understanding of the risks and dangers."

I started to speak at this point, but he cut me off. "We'll get to that in a minute. What I want to explain is this: ever since the Experiment began, the scientists at the center of it have been contemplating ways to alter history to make the twentieth century less bloody. That is the goal. It's both difficult and, at the same time, extremely easy since the bar is rather low. More than seventy million people died as a result of the Second World War, so even if they can't all be saved by our interventions, even altering history in ways that would save the lives of some of them would be an enormous victory."

"But—what do you mean by 'alter history'? What kind of—what did you call them—'interventions' are you talking about?"

"Altering history, as a concept, is fairly straightforward. We send our volunteers—people like you, one of whom you may become if you choose—back to some point either before or during the war, and you take actions that would, if successful—and if nothing else is disturbed in the process—result in lives saved."

"Actions like what?"

"Well, that varies. And I can't tell you what all our volunteers are doing: much as with the Los Alamos project, secrecy is essential even amongst those working together on the Experiment. But we do have an assignment in mind for you."

"And what would that be?"

He paused for a moment, looking straight into my eyes. I met his gaze, feeling the weird conviction that if I turned away, he would vanish, and I would never see him again. I wasn't sure if I wanted that or not, so I kept looking right at him so he couldn't disappear.

"You'll learn that later if you choose to join this project. As I said, the choice is yours. And I want to be clear about the risks before you agree."

"What risks?"

"Time travel is still relatively new. We've had a few glitches—not many—but one or two people have had difficulty in carrying out their assignments. Being dropped down into a new time and place can be very confusing, and not everyone has the mental and spiritual fortitude to deal with it. Especially since, once you are sent back to the past, you will essentially be alone. In an emergency, you can contact me, but day to day you will be on your own, trying to carry out your work surrounded by people of that era who have no idea what you're trying to do—and no idea what's coming. That can be difficult."

I nodded mutely, still trying to figure out if this was an elaborate hoax or the result of my brain being over-fried at the end of dissertation season. But somehow, Gunther's words compelled me, even as what he was saying terrified me.

And yet, as scary as the things he described sounded, somewhere in the back of my head, a small voice was also asking, *Well, why not?*

I'd always been, or thought of myself as, a person who wanted to do good in the world in some way. Perhaps this was a trait I got from my mother. She'd worked as a nurse for forty years, in which time she'd done it all—healing the sick, consoling the suffering, delivering new babies into the world, and comforting the dying as they left it. Even as a child, I was enthralled by her stories about her patients and her interactions with them, and I'd felt a similar call to make the world better somehow.

It didn't take me long to rule out medicine as a career in any way, shape, or form, but the desire to help people who needed it had stayed with me even as I went to college and began to pursue my history studies. At school, I studied the stories of wars, disasters, famines, plagues, and just about anything else that had befallen unlucky people throughout the centuries. Maybe the process of doing so had depressed me too much to ponder how I could make a difference here and now, and I shelved my more altruistic impulses as I emerged into adulthood.

But while my eyes remained firmly fixed on getting my doctorate and becoming a professor, some part of me still yearned to be of service to the world in a more concrete and powerful way. To be more like my mother. And now I realized that perhaps these two impulses weren't mutually exclusive.

I had devoted my entire life to studying history for a reason. It fascinated me, but there was more to it than that. What history really meant to me, in its essence, was tragedy. There were the triumphant moments, of course—oh, what I would give to have been part of the enormous crowd in Trafalgar Square in London on May 8, 1945, celebrating the defeat of Nazi Germany—but overall, history was often the story of war, catastrophe, and death. Too many people dying, or suffering, from things they needn't have lived through if someone had been able to foresee and prevent the damage.

And now, was Gunther telling me that there was actually a chance to do that? To help stop probably the greatest tragedy in all human history from occurring? I wasn't sure I was convinced, but at the same time, his story was both too bizarre and too complex to be the fantasy of a madman. Almost against my will, I found myself believing him—but in truth, maybe I was only believing him because I wanted to believe the world could be made better, its darkest moments scrubbed away, leaving the pages of history fresh and clean.

Or maybe I'm just a sucker. Or maybe I was using this opportunity as a subconscious way to put off my academic job search. I'm still not honestly sure of my motivations, but I do know that, after a few more minutes of Gunther's explanations, I had made up my mind.

I took a deep breath and spoke the words that would change my life forever.

"Yes. I'll do it."

4

GOING BACK

It was two days later when Gunther and I met for the second time, which was almost long enough for me to begin to doubt his existence. Once he'd left my house and I'd returned to catching up on dissertation writing, the encounter that had felt so compelling at the time began to seem like pure fantasy, my mind playing tricks. I'd been stressed out lately, I reasoned, and stress can do very strange things to the brain. Maybe I'd imagined it all. Perhaps I was on the verge of a nervous breakdown. That was far less scary than the alternative, in a way.

But any hopes I'd had that Gunther was a dissertation-induced hallucination vanished promptly at 8 p.m. that Sunday night when he appeared at my door and walked into my tiny living room without ceremony. He got right down to business.

"So, Vivienne, we're pleased you've decided to join the Experiment. I have an assignment for you, which I'll explain tonight."

I nodded, trying to look much cooler than I felt.

"Every person we select for participation in the Experiment is chosen because they have a specific skill set. Each can be useful in different ways."

"How can I be useful? What are my special skills?" All I could think of was writing and historical research, and I really didn't see how many lives that could save.

"I'll answer your first question in a moment. As to your skills, I would think that would be fairly obvious to you. What were you doing when we met?"

"Umm . . . writing my dissertation?"

"Exactly." He nodded as if that explained everything, though it clearly did not. "You are a historian, specializing in the Second World War, with a particular emphasis on England and Germany in the immediate pre-war period."

I nodded. I didn't bother to ask how he knew this. After all, the focus of my dissertation wasn't a secret; it was just that I couldn't imagine why anyone would go to the trouble to find out what it was. I'm pretty sure even my parents were tired of hearing about it by this point.

"So, that answers your question. Your special skill, which you've spent years cultivating and developing, is your knowledge of this particular period in history."

"That's it?" I couldn't help feeling a bit disappointed. "I mean—you picked me just because I know a lot about history?"

He looked at me severely. "That knowledge, you will soon find out, is an invaluable asset. Consider this: you are going to be sent back to a time in the past in which none of the people around you know this history, because for them, it's not history. It's the future. There is no possible way they could know the details of it. Not even the most powerful men in the world—the ones who are actually shaping the events that are happening around you—know what you know."

"But, I mean, surely a lot of people know the history of the Second World War? I mean, at least the basics?"

"You'd be surprised how little most people know about the conflict, considering how recent it was and how much of an impact it has had on the world ever since. And general knowledge is not enough. We need to send back people with detailed knowledge of events, because once you are in the past, there's no way you can find out what's going to happen. There's no internet to research any fact you may want to know, and even if it existed back then, it would have been useless since the things you'll need to know about haven't happened yet. You need to rely solely on your own knowledge and memory. In that sense, you have an edge over just about anyone else we could have chosen to carry out this work."

I nodded. What he said did make sense, even if it was surprising. Who ever thought the graduate student historians would be the ones to save the world?

"Okay, I see. And when you say 'this work,' what do you mean exactly?"

"Your assignment. Yes. That's what I'm here to discuss with you tonight; to give you the outline of your task and your instructions."

I nodded, waiting for him to proceed.

Gunther spoke for several minutes, explaining the task he—or whoever was behind the Experiment—had in mind for me. I listened for as long as I could without breaking in, but finally I couldn't stop myself.

"So, the whole assignment is to rescue children?"

"Precisely. Millions of children were killed in the Second World War—whether in concentration camps, in bombings, or when their countries were invaded. This is not only tragic in and of itself, but it represents an enormous loss of future potential. Who is to say what those children might have done, what they might have contributed to the world, had they been able to live out normal lifespans?"

I nodded thoughtfully. He was right, of course, even if I couldn't help thinking his focus on the children's "potential," rather than, as he perfunctorily noted, the tragedy of their deaths in and of themselves, was a bit cold-blooded.

"We want you to use your time in the past to save the lives of as many children as possible. Your particular focus will be on rescuing Jewish children in Germany, but you are not limited by this. We make no distinction as to the value of a life. If you can save a German child, do it. A British child, the same. The goal is to save as many as you can in the time you have."

"You mean I'm not going to get any more specific instructions? What do I do exactly, land in 1939 Germany and start asking all the Jewish parents to give me their children to take back with me to the future?"

"No, you misunderstand. You aren't taking these children to the present day, but simply to somewhere in their own time where they will be safe—or as safe as possible. Once you've had time to complete this assignment, we will bring you back here, to this exact date."

"But—" I was still baffled and had many more questions that I suspected Gunther might not answer. But I ploughed ahead regardless. "So, what you're saying is, I'm on my own to figure out how to do all of this?"

He regarded me wryly. "I will give you more specific details once you have been sent back. Anything I don't tell you explicitly, you will be able to figure out on your own. Knowing what you know and understanding the urgency of the task you face should motivate you."

I did not find this comforting. The idea of being dropped into the past, completely on my own except for occasional contact with a vaguely defined government entity, was intimidating enough. The prospect that children's lives hung on my ability to "figure it out" was close to terrifying.

I looked at Gunther and could tell from his expression that he had given me all the information he was going to share for now. Even if things were cloaked in mystery, at least I had a goal, an important one—far more important than knocking out the last two thousand words of my dissertation. All my life, I'd wanted to be truly useful in some way, to make the world better, and this was my chance. I was determined that I wasn't going to blow it.

However, I had one last pressing question, which I decided to ask even if Gunther wouldn't provide me with an answer.

"Um . . . I don't want to sound like I'm telling you your business here, but it seems there's a pretty obvious way to stop the bloodshed of the Second World War before it happens."

He regarded me coolly. "And what would that be?"

I couldn't believe I had to spell it out, but apparently, he was going to make me. "Why don't you just send back an assassin to kill Hitler before he rises to power in the first place?"

He nodded, a touch ruefully. "Of course, that would seem an obvious solution to you. One simple adjustment to the course of history that can fix everything in a single swoop. The reality, however, is a bit more complicated."

"Why is that?"

"Two reasons. For one thing, we don't know what such an enormous change in the arc of history would lead to. It could upend the world's course so completely that it could lead to even greater tragedy and bloodshed.

"For example," he said, raising his hand as I began to protest, "suppose Hitler were to be disposed of early enough that his regime never comes to pass. Do you think there are no other unsavory tyrants who could rise in his place, in Germany or elsewhere? And suppose that different decisions made by one of them resulted in another country managing to create the atomic bomb before America could do so—and using it in a far more destructive way?"

I shook my head. "Of course, that's a possibility, and I understand you'd need to be cautious, but come on. It's almost certain that killing Hitler before he can seize power would result in a far better world than one in which he starts a war that kills tens of millions of people. A hypothetical shouldn't stop you from trying when the stakes are so high!"

"You may well be right. However, for the moment, it remains impossible, whether it would be prudent to try or not."

"I don't understand."

"Time travel is, as I'm sure you can imagine, an incredibly complex and delicate scientific endeavor. There's a reason it took mankind until 1976 to invent it. And even after more than thirty years, it remains a work in progress. The science hasn't yet been perfected to the extent we hope to see one day. There remain limits to what we can do."

"What do you mean? What kind of limits?"

He reached into his pocket and pulled out a rubber band, then wrapped it around his fingers.

"As I said, the science is complex, far too complex for you to understand. Think of time travel in this way. See how my hands are placed together inside this rubber band? When I move them from their starting point—which we'll say is the current year, 2009—I can stretch the band out wider." He did so. "But as you can see, it will only stretch so far."

I shook my head. "So, what does that mean?"

"It means that we have the ability to travel through time now—but only so far. There are limits to how far we can move. This band"—he nodded at his hands—"can stretch forward from 1976 to 2014, and backward to 1938. But it cannot go any further in either direction."

"Why?"

"We don't know exactly why. However, these are the limits our technology has come up against. Whenever we have tried to send someone on an assignment further in the past, or into the future beyond 2014, we have failed."

I shuddered a bit, wondering what failure in those circumstances would look like, but decided not to ask.

"Eventually we hope to transcend these limits, but for now, it appears we can only move forward or backward about forty years from our starting point. So, regarding the Second World War, we can only go back to a year before it begins. Which makes an assassination attempt on Hitler difficult, to say the least. If we could travel back ten, or even five years earlier—we might have more luck. But to kill a world leader of a militant country on the eve of his beginning a war is not an easy task. Such people do not have their guard down often, and they are closely watched and protected."

I sighed and shook my head. There was always a catch, I supposed. I looked at Gunther and nodded my understanding. I was ready to begin.

Gunther stood up and removed from his pocket a small object no bigger than a paper clip. It was silver and shiny and seemed to glimmer mysteriously, as if it might vanish before my eyes.

"Umm—is that the time machine?" I'd been picturing something bigger—if not a DeLorean, at least something I could step into.

Gunther shrugged. "If it helps you to think of it that way, fine. Time travel is a bit of an abstract concept, I'm afraid. But when you touch this for ten seconds, you will be transported back to your destination."

"And where is that exactly? I mean, where and when?"

"Seventy years ago today, which would be April 14, 1939. Four and a half months before the war begins, which should give you time to get your work done before the conflict breaks out. As to location, we drop all our new arrivals in Trafalgar Square in London. It's usually so busy that nobody notices when a new person pops up there."

I pondered this for a moment, then nodded. "Okay. I'm ready."

I wasn't ready, not really. Three days ago, I'd been a grad student crashing on a deadline, and now I was about to become a time traveler. How could you truly be ready for something like that? But I consoled myself, or tried to, with the thought that surely none of the other people who'd been sent back by Gunther had been ready either, but they'd managed to survive, hadn't they?

"Excellent. Then go ahead and touch this for ten seconds. Once you've arrived, go to the red house at Number

12, Somerset Lane. You will receive another visit in a few days. And—I really cannot stress this enough, Vivienne— try to remain inconspicuous at first. Don't draw too much attention to yourself. And be very, very cautious about whom you speak to and interact with. And of course, discussing the Experiment with anyone from the time you are being dropped into is strictly forbidden. When trying to change history, it's best not to make waves."

He smiled a trifle grimly, then held out his hand. The paper-clip-sized object glimmered silver in his palm. Before I could change my mind or lose my nerve, I reached out, touched it, closed my eyes, and counted backwards from ten.

When I reached zero, I opened my eyes.

5

LONDON

Trafalgar Square, London, England
April 14, 1939

Buzzing.

My ears were still ringing as I opened my eyes, but slowly the sensation stopped, and I began to feel steadier. The buzzing sound was now emanating from the crowd around me rather than from my own head—and the effects of hurtling back in time seven decades.

I looked around, taking in my surroundings. I was in a spot I'd stood in many times before. I'd lived in London for a year while working on my dissertation, so the center of the city was familiar to me. I immediately recognized the statue of Admiral Horatio Nelson in the center of Trafalgar Square. I was standing far from the center, off on the side where, in *my* Trafalgar Square, the Caffé Nero coffeeshop would have been. There was no café there now, but instead what looked like might be a building filled with flats.

The square was filling up. Based on the sun, it was around noon, so it wasn't surprising that the plaza was getting packed. People hurried by, probably on their way to lunch, looking, at first glance, not too dissimilar from the harried London pedestrians I was used to seeing. Except that they wore hats and gloves. The women were all in dresses or skirts. And not a single person was glancing down at their phone.

Familiar, yet totally different. I'd entered the London of the 1930s. I felt dazed. The ringing sensation still lingered in my ears, and I was disoriented, even though I knew where I was. *You can do this*, I reminded myself. *In fact, you've trained your whole life for this, haven't you?* I straightened up, looking around to ensure that no one was staring at me. As Gunther had warned, I mustn't attract too much attention, at least not at the beginning.

I walked over to a young boy selling (hawking?) newspapers. I decided to buy one, reached into my pocket, and suddenly realized I didn't have any money. Well, that was quite an oversight! Why hadn't I considered I might need cash in my new destination? Why hadn't Gunther provided me with any? Oy. This Experiment was off to a splendid start.

Then I remembered Gunther's words: "*the red house at Number 12, Somerset Lane.*" I had to find that, and then, presumably, the rest of it would fall into place.

Ten minutes later, I had wound my way through side streets and arrived at Somerset Lane, number 12. But what now . . . Should I just walk in?

I walked up to the front step and knocked tentatively on the door.

It opened almost immediately, and I found myself looking at a plump, late-middle-aged woman with brown hair and eyes. She looked me over and seemed to be satisfied with my appearance.

"You're the new girl?" she asked.

"Um—yes, I guess I am. I've just arrived in London and was told to come here—"

She nodded her understanding, stepped back from the door, and gestured for me to enter. "Come in. I was told you'd be arriving today. Come along, I'll show you the flat."

Wordlessly, I followed her up three flights of stairs to a hallway with several doors along the corridor. She stopped at the second one, turned a key, and swung it open.

"Here it is. This is the flat I was told to hold for you to come look at. What do you think, Miss—so sorry, what is your name?"

"Vivienne."

"Vivienne, of course. Take a look around. If it's to your liking, you can move right in as soon as you want. Old tenants just moved out, and I'm looking to fill it quickly."

I walked around the room and took it in: a small space, with a bed in a corner, a tiny kitchen area, and a desk with a chair. Not fancy but certainly good enough for me; it was roughly the size of my studio apartment back home. I nodded.

"Yes, this looks very nice. You said I can move in right away?"

"Of course. Your first and last month's rent and deposit have been paid, so that's taken care of. Rent is due first of every month for as long as you'd like to stay."

She smiled for the first time, and I registered her kindly expression. It was nice to feel any kind of welcome on this totally bizarre day, and I smiled back. "Thank you."

"Lovely. Come down and have some tea. Oh, where are my manners, I should have introduced myself. I'm Martha Sainsbury."

"Nice to meet you, Martha." Tea and a bit of company sounded wonderful right about now, and I followed her gratefully down the stairs to her flat.

———————

Ten minutes later. we were sitting at a round wooden table in her kitchen over steaming cups of strong black tea and scones and cream she had thoughtfully provided to go with them.

"I've been landlady here for twenty years," she said, in answer to my question. "My husband bought this place a few years before the Great War, and we've rented it out ever since. Once he died, God rest him, I took over the management."

"And how did you know I was coming?" I was curious how these pieces seemed to be falling into place since Gunther hadn't prepared me with much advance detail.

"The company you work for—Experimental Limited, aren't they called?—usually keeps a room here for their girls. Typists mostly, and stenographers. Is that what you do?"

"Yeah, more or less."

"And you're American, I take it? I can tell by your accent."

"Yes, I am."

She shook her head, apparently in wonder. "Never been there. Is it nice?"

I nodded. "Yes. But I love England too. I used to live here, a few years ago, when I was at university. And my mom is English."

"Really? Where is she from?"

"A little town called Stratfield. It's not too far from London." I figured it couldn't hurt to tell the truth about myself as much as possible, since it wasn't likely any of the people I met would be able to fact-check me and discover that my mother had yet to be born, and my time living in England wouldn't happen for another sixty-five years or so. The fewer lies and cover details I had to keep straight, the better.

"Ah. Yes, I think I've heard of it. Anyway, welcome to the flat. As I said, you can start moving in your things whenever you like."

"Great, thanks. I don't have much stuff with me." That was an understatement! And it reminded me, yet again, that I had no money with me either. As if reading my mind (hopefully not) Martha suddenly put down her cup of tea and reached for something on the table behind her. She handed me a large envelope.

"I almost forgot—your company asked me to give you this. I gather it's to cover your expenses while you're in London. How long will that be?"

I quickly tore open the envelope and glanced through the contents. Without counting it out, I could see there should be enough money here, at 1930s prices, to sustain me for a while. I was a bit surprised they'd trusted Martha with so much money, but then again, she seemed an honest sort. And I could only assume Experimental Ltd had already done their research on her.

I stood up, and she rose, too, as I pondered her last question. "I'm not really sure. I'll let you know when my job here is done."

The question, I reflected, was how I would know that.

6

ANDREW

After tea with Martha, I headed out to wander through London. I wanted to see the city and get a feel for it again, and I also needed to buy just about everything.

Several hours later I was back at my new flat, lugging with me bags containing clothes, shoes, toiletries, and some basic food items. I wondered how much eating out regularly in 1939 London would cost me; I'd never been much of a cook. My favorite meal to make at home was avocado toast, and I doubted avocados were readily available in English markets now.

I tried to turn the key while struggling with several of the bags, when suddenly I heard a deep voice behind me, "Hullo, need a bit of help?"

I turned around and may have gasped a bit. I was looking into the face of a young man—my age, maybe, or a few years younger—with dark hair and eyes and a friendly, open expression I wasn't used to seeing on the faces of strangers in London. He was very handsome, almost ridiculously so, and dressed in what I immediately recognized as a Royal Air Force uniform.

"Um . . . Yes, I guess I do." I smiled tentatively as he swiftly removed two of the bags from my arms, enabling me to focus on jiggling the key in the lock. The door swung open, creaking a bit on its hinges. "Thank you so much."

"Not at all." He smiled at me, the sort of smile I would probably have described as "heart-melting" if I were sufficiently prone to sap. But I can't deny that it made me feel something powerful, as if something inside me were shifting in a way I couldn't really explain. "I'm Vivienne."

"Nice to meet you, Vivienne. Been shopping, I take it?"

"Yes, I have. I'm just moving in. Furnishing my new house, you see."

"Ah. Looks like we're to be neighbors, then. I live in the flat down the hall." He gestured behind him.

"Oh, good." Very good. Very, very good. Get it together, Vivienne, and don't blow this. "Well, thanks again for helping me. Can I offer you some tea?" That felt sufficiently English for an introduction.

He smiled, nodding. "Sounds good. Thanks awfully." Then he said apologetically, "So sorry, I forgot to introduce myself. I'm Andrew Sheffield."

"Nice to meet you, Andrew." I motioned for him to follow me into the flat, where I put down my bags and hoped fervently there might be some tea left in the shelves from the last tenant, as I'd just realized I didn't have any. Fortunately, I was in London and my quick search did not disappoint; I soon brought out some loose tea and teacups and located a kettle. "Please sit down."

"Thank you. Nice place you've got here." He glanced around at its sparse interior. "Never been inside before."

"Oh? You weren't friendly with the last tenants?"

"Not really. Passed them by every now and again in the hall and nodded, but nothing more than that."

A few minutes later the tea was ready, and I quickly prepared two cups for us. My mother would be proud that her training in tea-making hadn't gone to waste, even though I hadn't used this skill in years.

"Cheers." Andrew accepted his mug, took a sip, and smiled again. He looked at me with interest, searchingly, almost as if he were waiting for something.

So, I guess now would be a good time to mention a little fact about myself: I've always had a thing for RAF pilots. When I was a teenager and first began studying World War II, I spent hours reading historical novels that featured the brave, dashing, heroic, young British pilots who had fought in the skies against the Germans, and, for me, this became the archetype of my fantasy man. Other girls were entranced by rock singers or movie stars, but all I wanted was a pilot: a glory boy, heading off to fight the Nazis and save the world. The only problem was that, for what I was seeking, I'd been born about sixty years too late.

Except now, here I was. And here was an actual RAF pilot, every bit as charming and captivating as the ones

I'd been fantasizing about since I was thirteen. And maybe, since we were both in the same time and place, however briefly, there was finally a chance for my fantasy to come true?

I shook my head quickly to bring myself back to the present—or what was currently my present. It was all becoming very confusing, and I thought of Gunther's warnings about the challenges of living in a time that wasn't one's own. I wondered where he was now, and when I would see him again.

But I pushed those thoughts aside and turned my attention back to Andrew, who was telling me about himself: he was from a small town in Sussex, in the south of England; he had graduated from Oxford five years ago; he'd joined the RAF last year after working for a few years teaching history at a small college near his hometown.

"Wow, quite a career change," I commented, putting down my tea and giving Andrew my full attention again. "What made you decide to become a pilot?"

"Yes, I expect it does sound rather odd, doesn't it?" He smiled ruefully and shrugged. "I wanted to serve my country. The darker things have become on the Continent these past few years, the more I've felt that something's coming, something big, and we need to be prepared when it does. This is the best way I know to help. If war comes, I want to be able to be of some use. I want to fight for England."

"Do you think war will come?" I asked him tentatively.

He nodded. "Since Munich, yes, I do. I don't know when. But I do think it's inevitable, sooner or later. And I know most people don't like to hear that; it's easier to go on about our lives and ignore the signs, the possibilities..."

"The gathering storm," I murmured, thinking of Winston Churchill.

He smiled at me, his expression quizzical. "Yes, that's right. Brilliant way of putting it. That's exactly how it feels. You have a way with words, Vivienne."

I felt the shame of my unintentional plagiarism and shook my head. "Oh, that's just an expression a friend of mine uses sometimes. Don't give me any credit for it."

"And what about you? You're from the States, clearly... I can tell from your accent. What brings an American girl to London these days?"

"I've just been hired for a new job," I replied smoothly. I had to repeat this often enough to make it convincing, and the fewer details, the better. "It's a temporary thing, but I'll be in London for a while to do the work. That's why I've rented the flat."

"I see. First time in London?"

"No, I studied here at university for a bit."

"Oh, really? What did you study?"

"History."

He gave me a penetrating glance, seeming to size me up. "Very interesting. I'd love to hear more about it, but unfortunately, I've got to go now—officer's meeting, and I mustn't be late. But I hope I'll see you around again, Vivienne?" He smiled, stood up, and took my hand in his. My stomach contracted, and I felt sensations vibrating around inside me that I hadn't experienced in a very long time. The life of an academic can be a lonely one; the work is consuming and often solitary. But perhaps now things would be different: a new job, a new era, a new life.

"Yes," I managed to reply casually. "I'll be here."

At least for the foreseeable future, I thought to myself as I walked him to the door and watched him walk down the hall, waving as he reached the building's front door. *I'll be here, until I'm not.* I simply had no idea how long that would be.

7

THE PUB

After Andrew left, I began to feel a bit lonely. It was quiet in the flat, and no one else seemed to be home; I wasn't sure where Martha was. The emptiness of the building started to wear on me a bit, and it struck me for the first time that there was literally no one I could talk to, until or unless Gunther made a reappearance. Every single person I'd ever known—my family, my friends, my colleagues at school—were not only not here in London, they hadn't even been born yet. The people already living here had their own lives, no doubt, and I had no place in them. I felt like an immigrant to a new land, which I suppose I was, but this was a very different feeling than when I'd moved to London as a student. For the first time, I felt intensely aware that I was in a place where I did not belong.

Well, there was nothing to do about that, I told myself. I have an assignment, I'll carry it out, and then I'll go back. Of course, I still had no idea exactly what the details of my assignment were, but I remembered Gunther's words, "You will receive another visit in a few days." That would hopefully clear things up. As this was only mid-April, I still had nearly five months before the war would begin, which should buy me some time to figure it all out.

In the meantime, I told myself, I should treat this as a bit of a combination sabbatical and vacation. I was back in the era I'd spent my entire adult life studying, in the city that had been the focus of most of my research; I might as well take advantage of this extraordinary opportunity. I grabbed my newly purchased rain slicker and umbrella (because I was in London) and headed outside for a walk.

I walked a long way—down to Trafalgar Square, through Whitehall, to Westminster Abbey, and past Buckingham Palace. After stopping for a rest in Green Park, my favorite London open space, I ambled over to the Embankment and the Thames River.

Darkness had fallen while I'd been wandering around, and I now saw the London panorama lit up and spread out in front of me, like a vision of lost beauty. I remembered how many times I'd walked this way, taken in these same views, which seemed not much different than in my student days. I felt an ache for that past, for how simple it now seemed. But that past—my past—still lay in the future. And before I could stroll these streets as a carefree American girl in the early twenty-first century, London still had to get through the twentieth.

It was April 1939. I reminded myself of that simple fact as if I were resetting a clock in my head for a new time zone. Five more months until the war would begin—the war that some, like Andrew, were clearly gearing up for but most of the people around me were still happily oblivious to. Oh, I'm sure they had some concerns, some fears. But denial is powerful, as the run-up to the Second World War proved. Things were looking gloomy now, but no grief had befallen London yet. Maybe it wouldn't.

Except it would. I knew that. Somewhere out there, on the continent of Europe, men were making plans to start a conflict that would lead to a global conflagration—and a holocaust so horrific that we later capitalized it and studied it in our schools. Never again, we swore solemnly, although we had already failed several times to keep that noble promise. But again, that was the future, rendered seemingly inevitable by the past I was now living in, my new present. The people around me didn't know what was coming, but I did.

It was a very strange feeling, and I began to shiver as I gazed around the peaceful London panorama I knew so well. I knew the timeline in my head perfectly: less than five months from now, the war would begin. By this time next year, the "phony war" would end with Hitler's invasion of Norway, and a month later, France would fall. The

British would rescue their army through the "Miracle of Dunkirk" that June, but by September 1940, German bombs would begin falling on London, on this very ground where I now stood. Fifty-seven straight nights of fire would rain down on the city from above. Amazingly, the British people never gave up. Thank God.

I looked around at the handful of nighttime strollers around me. It had begun to rain, and was well after 9 p.m., so there weren't too many people out here with me, but there were a few. I looked at them and tried to think my way into their minds. I wondered how many of them would still be alive in a few years, after the war ended. Most would, but certainly not all. And every one of them would suffer terrors I couldn't even begin to imagine, having grown up when I did. I felt that they were somehow different from me, as if they were another type of human: more stoic, more resilient. I, in comparison, was a spoiled, shallow child, whose safety in the world of the future had been bought through the steep cost of their sacrifices.

And I was different in another way. I knew what was coming, not just to England, but to the tens of millions of people who would perish in the Second World War, on the doorstep of which the world now lingered. Gas chambers and crematoriums not yet in existence would soon be built to dispose of millions of human beings, as simply and efficiently as tossing out the garbage. It was something I had never been able to wrap my head around in all my time studying this era, and I wondered if the people strolling past me, breathing in this damp, rainy London air, were even capable of conceiving of it. *The banality of evil, man's inhumanity to man.* However one phrased it, the Second World War had ushered in a new reality, in which mankind's capacity for monstrous acts was laid bare, never again able to be denied by those who would come after. I understood things about human nature that these people couldn't, because they hadn't yet crossed the red line in time that would reveal the darkest crimes in human history. How would they feel when they did?

The rain began to fall harder; soon it was pouring. My existential musings had thoroughly depressed me, and I needed a drink. Wandering through the streets, I soon came upon a pub that looked promising: brightly lit from within by golden light. I stepped inside gratefully, shaking out my umbrella and grabbing a seat near the window to watch the rain fall. I walked up to the bar, ordered a lager, and took it back to my table. Within a few minutes I'd emptied it, and a young woman, dressed in a waitress's uniform, passed by me holding a tray.

"Care for another round, miss?" She was dark-haired and pale, with a lovely porcelain complexion, and the lilt in her accent sounded Irish. I nodded my thanks, and within a few minutes she had brought me another lager. Service here was surprisingly attentive, I thought.

"Thanks," I said as she put the drink down. She smiled, and I noticed how pretty she was; her eyes were hazel, her skin flawless. She swept back to the bar, and I wondered briefly how an Irish girl had come to be in England at this point in history. Feeling curious—and also, I must admit, rather lonely—I wandered up to the bar, hoping for a bit of a chat. The pub had been fairly crowded when I entered, with people escaping the rain, but it had now emptied out, and there were plenty of seats available. The young waitress, or barmaid, came over to me and inquired, "One more for you?"

"No, thanks, I should probably stop at two if I'm going to find my way home." She smiled again, and I asked, "Excuse me, but if you don't mind my asking, where are you from?"

Her mouth wrinkling up a bit, she replied, "Well, I live in South London now. But County Kerry is my home."

"Oh, really?" I asked, intrigued. "My family comes from Kerry too."

She looked surprised. "But you certainly don't sound Irish, not with your accent. American, aren't you?"

"Yes, I am. But my mother's family is English, and her parents came over here from Ireland years ago."

"Ah," she nodded. "'Tis a beautiful country. I miss it often." She looked around as she said this, as if afraid someone at the bar would catch her sounding ungrateful.

"It certainly is," I agreed. "I've visited a few times."

She was looking at me with curiosity. "But you're American? What brings you here from the States?"

"Just some work I'm doing in London," I replied, and hastily changed the subject. "What about you? What brought you to London?"

She smiled, though her eyes looked rather sad. "I came for a job. Hard to find work in Kerry. And the man I'm to marry lives here. He came over just a few months before I arrived, then he sent for me."

"Ah," I said. "Well, congratulations on your upcoming marriage."

She nodded her thanks, smiled again briefly, and returned to the bar.

I finished my drink and decided to head back to the flat, hoping I'd be able to find my way in the dark. Before I left, I stole a look back at the young waitress. She looked familiar, somehow, though that was obviously impossible. Perhaps my loneliness was making me seek out attachments to total strangers, to try to see something recognizable in their faces.

She caught my eyes and smiled. I smiled back, shook out my umbrella, and headed back out into the rain.

―――――――――――

When I finally reached my flat, I felt exhausted, thoroughly drained by my lengthy ramble around London and all the existential musings that had accompanied me during my walk. The two drinks I'd consumed at the pub hadn't been enough to give me any kind of happy alcohol buzz; if anything, they'd sunk me deeper into gloom. And loneliness.

As I walked through the front door, shaking my still-sopping umbrella, I wondered where Andrew was now and what he was doing. My thoughts kept returning to him after our single encounter. It was almost too perfectly arranged; I travel back in time to the Second World War and instantly meet a dashing pilot, destined no doubt to be a hero in the apocalyptic conflict that was about to unfold. Of course, he didn't know that yet. No one around me knew, for certain, what the future would bring them so soon. But wasn't that always the way of life? Of course. Back home, I had no idea what fate awaited me in 2010 or 2020 or 2050. But how often did I think about that, or let it bother me? The honest answer was—practically never. I just went about my days, planning for the future as best I could, but hardly expecting that at any point that future could reach up and swallow me and all of my hopes and dreams like some invisible monster.

Still, given Andrew's reasons for joining the RAF, and his clearsighted views of what the next few years might hold for England, it was obvious he was more perceptive than most. He'd looked into the abyss of what fate might bring, and instead of choosing to hide from it, he'd instead made the decision to change his life in order to meet it. That took a special kind of bravery. I couldn't help admiring him, even though I barely knew him. At least, not yet.

"Hullo, Vivienne." I looked up in surprise; I had thought I was alone given the silence of the house, but here was Martha Sainsbury, the landlady I'd chatted with earlier today. I recovered myself and smiled at her.

"Hello, Mrs. Sainsbury. How are you?"

"I'm fine, thank you. Are you just getting back?"

I wondered for a brief second if she was going to turn out to be a typical nosy landlady, listening to creaks in my floor to tell if I was home or out enjoying myself instead.

But then she smiled, a bit hesitantly, and I softened. I wondered what her life was like, if perhaps she sometimes felt lonely too.

"Yes, I just went out for a walk. And then stopped into a pub," I added, feeling compelled to be truthful. There was a motherly air about Martha that made it difficult to lie to her.

"Well, it looks like you got caught in the rain. Not as much of that in the States, I imagine? Would you like a cup of tea?"

"I'd love one," I said gratefully, thinking that a warm cup of anything sounded like heaven right now.

Martha ushered me into her parlor and begin preparing the tea. She also brought out some shortbread biscuits, even though it wasn't strictly teatime. I suspected I was going to like her.

"Thank you," I said as she put the steaming cup in front of me, and I took a sip. "This is perfect on a day like today."

She nodded, setting down her own cup of tea. "You're quite welcome. Nice to have your company."

"How many people live in your house?" I asked curiously.

"Oh, usually just a few at a time. The house has six rooms, but only three are filled at the moment, including yours."

"Do you enjoy being a landlady?" I asked, instantly thinking it a stupid question. But she nodded, apparently unfazed.

"I do. It keeps me busy, and the work has been a blessing since my husband died, God rest him." She shook her head and began rocking back and forth in her chair.

"Do you have any children?" I asked, hoping I wasn't prying too deeply, but feeling compelled to keep asking questions. I still felt a bit hungry for human contact and conversation after the day I'd had.

"I do. My daughter lives in Surrey with her husband and children. I don't get to see them too often. My son, Edward, was killed in the war."

"I'm so sorry," I murmured, taken aback. Of course, millions of young men had been killed during World War I, so this news wasn't surprising, but it still felt almost unreal to speak with a parent who'd actually been bereaved in that awful conflict. I wondered how old Martha was—sixty-five, seventy? If she were seventy, she'd have been born in 1869, just a few years after the end of the American Civil War, and more than a hundred years before me. And yet here we were, through a miracle of top-secret technology I still couldn't begin to understand, sitting in her kitchen, talking about her lost son. It occurred to me that Martha was the oldest person I'd ever met in my life.

She nodded, still rocking back and forth in her chair. "He was killed in 1916. In the Battle of the Somme."

I closed my eyes, trying to picture it; a young man, barely more than a boy, who'd be middle-aged by now if he'd lived, suddenly struck down on the battlefield, in a war between an array of European monarchs, first cousins, that he'd never met. Foxholes, barbed wire, mustard gas, the first-ever use of machine guns—World War I had never been the focus of my studies, but it was the inevitable backdrop for the war I was studying so extensively.

It had led to the creation of a new, darker world—the world in which I was now living.

"I'm so very sorry," I said softly. "That's such a tragedy."

Martha nodded but didn't seem inclined to say anything more. Then she spoke again. "All those poor boys, those young men, who gave their lives—and for what, in the end? You tell me. I still don't know. I only hope and pray there will never be such a war again."

I looked down at my cooling tea, avoiding her stare. I felt guilty, though I knew I wasn't. I already knew her prayers were useless; that another, even worse war was destined to darken the world in a matter of months. I wondered how Martha would react when it arrived. Would she be shocked? Angry? Or stoic, determined to rise to the new occasion, to keep calm and carry on once again?

"I'm sorry, my dear," Martha said, and as I looked up, she was smiling slightly. "I'm sure this isn't the kind of chat you were hoping for, was it? Tell me a bit about yourself. What is America like?"

I smiled, grateful for the change of topic, and did my best to describe a version of 1939 America I'd only read about but never lived in. The lies would keep piling up, I could see, until the day I left this place. I might as well get in some practice telling them now.

8

THE SECOND VISIT

It was two nights later when Gunther showed up again. *Finally*, I thought. While I still had somewhat mixed feelings about him, at the moment he felt like a beacon of light in the midst of the darkness.

His reappearance was unceremonious. He simply showed up at my door one evening, knocking with a few impatient raps, after I'd spent a rainy day wandering around London's museums.

"Hello, Vivienne," he said without preamble. "I see you found the apartment."

"Yes." Feeling a bit piqued, I added, "A few more details about where I was supposed to go wouldn't have hurt, you know."

"Yes, well, in any case you seem to have settled in. Good. Now, let's discuss your assignment."

"So, you are going to give me more details? I don't have to figure it out all by myself?" I was straining hard to keep the irritation, even anger, out of my voice, mostly because I was afraid if I blew up at him, he might vanish and leave me completely adrift in this time and place for eternity.

He sat down and handed me a piece of paper and something which, on closer inspection, turned out to be a train ticket. Round trip, from London to Berlin. The departure date was tomorrow at 11 a.m.; the return was for two days later.

"Here is what you will do next. Tomorrow, you will travel to Berlin. You can take the eleven o'clock train from London to Dover. There's a ferry that runs from Dover to Calais, where you will again take the train that will eventually bring you to Germany. Pack lightly, just enough for a few days. Once you arrive, go to this address." He tapped the sheet of paper.

"And what do I do when I arrive? What is this place?"

"A house. You will find a woman waiting for you there—Frau Schroeder. In her home are several Jewish children whom we are planning to resettle in London before the war begins. They range in ages between eighteen months and four years. You are to collect them there, along with their papers, and bring them back to London two days later."

My head was spinning, and Gunther's matter-of-fact tone was not reassuring. He made the whole thing sound simple—an easy transaction—but I suspected it would be more complex than he was letting on.

"So, I meet this woman, she brings the children to me, and I take them back here? What about their parents?"

For the first time, I saw what looked like a flicker of emotion cross Gunther's face. "The parents will not be there. They have entrusted their children to Frau Schroeder on the promise that she will get them to safety before war breaks out, through you."

"They're giving their children away? To whom?"

"We have foster parents waiting for them here in England. You needn't concern yourself with that part. When you arrive in London, bring them to this address." He pointed to a second address lower on the page that I hadn't noticed before. "There will be someone waiting to pick them up and take them to their new families."

I sat back, pondering my assignment. It sounded so simple—simple and clean, a quick transfer of several small people from one home to another. But for the first time, the tragedy within the tragedy occurred to me; that parents were giving up their children to total strangers to keep them safe, without any assurance of what was to come. It felt wrong, unspeakably so, and I suddenly felt uneasy about my own part in it.

"Isn't there any way we could bring the parents along with the children? Settle the families in England?" I was pretty sure I knew the answer to that.

"British immigration laws, as they currently stand, won't permit that. The parents are not wealthy; they are working-class people who have no chance of getting out of Germany before the war starts, and once it begins, they will be trapped. They are seizing the opportunity to send their children to safety, to spare them from what is to come."

"But . . ." I paused. "I mean, you and I know what is to come, but they don't. Not for sure. Why are they willing to give their children away before the war even begins?"

"A good question, Vivienne. And this explains why there are only three children coming back with you on this trip. For several months now, we have been working with Frau Schroeder to arrange this trip—lining up false papers, securing transport, seeking out Jewish parents in Berlin who are willing to let their children go in order to save them. There aren't many. As you point out, they don't know what's coming, and it's very difficult to persuade mothers and fathers to give up their children on the speculation that they may be in danger in an uncertain future, when they can't even be sure that war will come. But a handful of them are far-sighted enough and have strong enough resolve and love for their children to seize the chance to get them out while they still can. That's where you come in. It's your job to help these parents—ordinary men and women, who are doing the most difficult thing a parent could be asked to do—get their children to safety."

I nodded solemnly. A part of me—an enormous part—hated this entire plan, even though I knew it was necessary. The curse of foresight, of knowing what was to come. But I realized I had to put my own feelings aside and do all I could to help.

"I'll go pack now," I said. "I'll be on the train tomorrow morning, and back here in a few days."

He almost smiled at me, for the first time I could recall. "Very good. I will return three days from now, once you've come back with the children and delivered them to their new homes. And in the meantime, you are to tell no one where you are going, what you are doing there, or why."

I nodded and showed him out the door, thinking I would be almost glad to see him again when he returned, if only because it would mean my assignment was over. Then I began to pack for my trip to Berlin.

9

BERLIN

As my train pulled into the station, I shivered. Here I was at last. Berlin, 1939. Just before it all began. I had a strange sensation as I stepped out of the train car and picked my way carefully through the station until I reached the street outside. I wouldn't exactly call it déjà vu, more like a sense that I had finally arrived in a place I was always destined to reach eventually. It was as if my whole life and all the myriad details that went into it had led up to this strange moment when I walked into the metaphorical lion's den.

I shook off these thoughts and glanced at the piece of paper still clutched in my right hand. *Just do your job*, I told myself. *Do it and come home.* Strange that I was already thinking of 1939 London as home, when I'd only been there a few days, but my tiny flat near Covent Garden suddenly felt like a paradise compared to this place.

Fortunately, it was only a few blocks' walk to the address I'd been given, and I tried to focus on finding the exact rendezvous spot and not looking suspicious in any way. No one gave me a second glance, but then, there was no reason they should. My blond hair, blue eyes, and newly purchased 1930s coat, hat, and gloves allowed me to fit in seamlessly with most of the people I passed; I was just another Aryan on her way to buy groceries, or pick up milk, or mail a letter, or whatever these people did to pass their days while waiting for the world to explode.

When I reached the door, I knocked quietly three times. I didn't have to wait long. A moment later, a dark-haired, heavyset woman stood at the door, arms folded, staring at me.

"Guten Tag, Frau Schroeder?" My rusty German appeared with a bit of prompting from the pits of my memory (I'd spent a summer studying in Munich years ago to access some archives that were essential to my dissertation research). I wasn't sure she *was* Frau Schroeder, though I imagined she was, so I tilted the last of my words up into a question. She nodded. "I've come from the house with the red door." That was the code; simple enough, and it worked like a charm. Frau Schroeder stepped back and waved me in. I stepped into the house.

It was a small flat, rather dimly lit but neatly maintained, not a pillow out of place in the front parlor. She led me back to a windowless room at the far end, where three small figures sat on a couch, fidgeting a bit but otherwise very quiet.

"Here are the children," she said without preamble. "That's Ernst"—she pointed to the one on the left—"that's Lieb, and the little one is Lillian." She pointed to the smallest child, the only girl, sitting on the end of the couch. They were all tiny, no older than three or four in my decidedly non-expert opinion, but Lillian was hardly more than a baby.

Frau Schroeder stood back and folded her arms, looking at me. She seemed to feel this brief introduction explained everything and that I would know what to do. And I did, strictly speaking: take these children with me, after collecting their false identity papers from her, get them on a train back to England, and pass them on for settlement into a new life. But suddenly, this series of relatively simple tasks seemed beyond me. They looked so lost, so fragile. I felt if I touched any of them, they might break. I'd never spent much time with kids before, as an only child who had never babysat, and now all I could think of was what these children had already been through, being taken from their parents' arms and given to a stranger—first Frau Schroeder, and now me. Who were we to be in charge of their lives and to decide their fates? But, I reminded myself, their fates had already been decided by their parents, who were entrusting the two of us with their children because it was the only hope they had of saving them from greater tragedy. And I knew the future and knew they were right. So, I would just have to get on with it.

I stepped forward, looked at all three children, and mustered a smile for them. "Hello," I said in German, "I'm very glad to meet you all. My name is Vivienne. I'm going to take you on a trip, and you'll get to ride a train today! Are you ready?"

None of them moved but kept staring at me as if waiting for some greater inducement. I thought hard. What would have motivated me at this age?

"And before we go on the train, maybe we can see if they sell ice cream at the train station. Would you like that?"

Ernst and Lieb looked at me as though I had pulled a rabbit out of a hat. Apparently, ice cream is the magic word for small children of any country, in any era. I took advantage of their dazzled expressions to reach forward and hold out my hand. Ernst looked down, then slowly entwined his tiny fingers with mine. After a moment of hesitation, Lieb nodded his agreement to proceed as well. Feeling a maternal instinct towards the youngest of the group, I reached over and picked up Lillian with my other arm. She was surprisingly heavy; I always forget how much kids can weigh. As if sensing my struggle, Frau Schroeder indicated the wall behind her, where a stroller was waiting. I carefully placed Lillian in it, then gave the boys a smile I hoped was encouraging, all the while praying that the Berlin train station would indeed have ice cream available. These kids had suffered more than enough already.

Frau Schroeder handed me an envelope, labeled "papers," which I quickly slipped into my shoulder bag. I nodded to her, not quite sure what to make of our encounter, but grateful for her help. Our small crew, holding hands and dreaming of ice cream and new beginnings, walked out the door into the gray, overcast Berlin afternoon.

10

THE BEGINNING OF SOMETHING BIG

I returned to my flat in London two days later, utterly exhausted. I had completed my first assignment with no major difficulties: gotten the children on the train, handed their false papers to the attendants who barely glanced at them before waving me impatiently on. I'd been worried about encountering more trouble, as smuggling Jewish children out of Nazi Germany didn't seem like it would be a walk in the park, but it was surprisingly simple, and things went as smoothly as I could have possibly hoped.

If anything, the hardest part had come when we reached London, and I had to turn the children over to the social worker who was in charge of getting them to their adoptive families. At least here there was no need for subterfuge, but by then I'd bonded much more than

I'd expected with the kids. Ernst, in particular, had turned out to be quite chatty, telling me about his favorite toys and dreams of one day having a dog. Lillian didn't say much—I don't know if she didn't yet have much vocabulary or was simply struck by sensory overload with everything that was happening to her—but her little hand never left mine when she toddled along unsteadily, and by the time I had to leave, she sobbed as if I were her own mother. I felt so guilty about leaving her that a part of me wondered desperately if I might be able to arrange to keep her with me instead of handing her over to yet another set of new parents, but I knew that wasn't the plan. I was not going to be here long-term and was hardly set up to take care of a child. Not exactly what the Experiment had in mind for me.

I wondered if I'd see Gunther again when I returned to my flat, but night began to fall, and there was no sign of him. I began to feel lonely and restless, especially with no one to talk to, and decided to take a walk. The weather was warm, the air sweetly perfumed by spring flowers. I felt like getting outside, so I grabbed my spring coat and headed for the door.

I was turning my key to lock it when I heard a man's voice behind me—not Gunther, but someone far more welcome. "Hullo there. On your way out?"

I spun around, and there was Andrew, my RAF pilot neighbor, smiling at me. He was out of uniform but only seemed to have grown more handsome since our first meeting. My heart thudded a bit, as if I were still engaged in a covert operation (though I suppose, technically, I indeed still was).

"Oh, hi there," I replied, nervously brushing my hair back from my face and smiling. "Yes, I was just going for a walk. And you?"

"Just getting in. Long day, I'm afraid." He shook his head. "Where are you walking?"

"I don't know. I guess I'll just wander around the neighborhood a bit. I love this area." I paused, then before I could reconsider, added, "Would you like to join me?"

He looked a bit surprised, then smiled more deeply. "Sure. I think a walk would do me good—been working inside all day today. I could use some exercise."

"Great," I replied, rather moronically. I waited a few minutes for him to drop his satchel in his flat, and then we headed out together into the warm London evening, to enjoy the calm before the storm.

Half an hour later, we were strolling through Green Park, enjoying the last bits of the day's light before night would fall. I glanced over at Buckingham Palace and wondered if the King and Queen were inside right now, and what young Elizabeth and Margaret might be up to. Imagining Queen Elizabeth, that majestic, elderly icon of British royalty who'd been around my entire life, as a thirteen-year-old girl was a bit mind-bending, but at this moment, she was indeed thirteen. Don't ever let anyone tell you time travel won't mess with your head, especially if you are already prone to overthinking everything.

"So, you're settling in all right?" Andrew asked me.

"Oh, yes," I replied automatically, not sure if I was being truthful or not. "I love London."

"And your new job is going well?"

I shrugged. "Fine so far. I mean, a job's a job, right?"

He smiled. "I suppose so. Does your job have to do with your studies? I mean, is it about history?"

I nodded, hoping he wouldn't probe much more deeply. If I was going to get to know him well (hopefully so), I realized I would need a more elaborate cover story about my work to explain my presence in London. Maybe it was just snobbery, but I didn't want him to think I was a stenographer.

Actually, I don't think it was snobbery. Looking back, as I recall that evening, I think I could already tell that something was brewing here between Andrew and myself, and it made me loathe to lie to him, even if I wouldn't be able to tell him the whole truth. I wanted him to like me. And for that to happen, I would have to let him see *me* as much as I possibly could.

He dropped the subject of work for the time being, which was a relief. I decided to turn the conversation back to him, usually a safe bet with a man, as long as he's interesting enough that you want to listen to the result.

"So, Andrew, what do you like to do for fun?"

"Fun?" He grinned, looking rather boyish. "To be honest, I don't have much time for that these days. But I read a lot. Play a bit of rugby with my friends sometimes when I have a free day. And every now and then, I like a pint at the local."

"Really? Where's your local? I'm still figuring out the neighborhood."

"I can take you there if you like. I think you'll like it. Best beer in all the land."

"Really?"

"Ah, I guess not. But I tell myself that to justify the money I spend there."

I smiled. "I'd love to go. Do we still have time?"

"Sure. It won't close for a bit. Just down this street a few minutes; I'll lead the way."

He took my arm lightly as he said this, as if to guide me in the right direction. It felt like a delightfully unnecessary move, a signal.

I gave him a smile that was an agreement to proceed, feeling happier than I had since arriving in London. Thoughts of war, Berlin, and sorrowful parents and their lost children left me for a moment, or at least lifted. Something about Andrew made me feel lighter, happier than I felt like I had any right to be in this time and place. When we'd first met, I'd thought it might be fun to have a fantasy-fulfilling fling with him, but already I could feel that my emotions were changing into something deeper. I felt as if I needed him to survive here, like a plant needs oxygen to grow in a dark forest. Crazy, I know, since this was only our second conversation. But then, it was no crazier than anything else I'd experienced in the past few weeks. And really, love is always a bit crazy, isn't it?

In my experience, yes.

Andrew led me through the streets and a short time later, we were standing outside his local, which looked surprisingly familiar. "I know this place!" I blurted.

"You do?"

"Yes. I mean, I've only been here once." It was the very pub I'd ducked into the day I'd arrived in London of 1939, seeking refuge from the rain.

He held the door open for me, and we walked in and found a booth in the back. "I usually sit at the bar," Andrew said, "and have a chat with the bartender. But this way we'll have a bit more privacy." He smiled.

A moment later, the pretty, dark-haired Irish waitress I'd talked to on my first visit was at our table, smiling as she readied herself to take our order. She looked first at Andrew, then at me, and the recognition dawned on her face. "Hello there, Andrew. What'll it be?"

"Just a lager, thanks. And for you?" He turned to me.

"The same, thanks." I didn't feel like exposing my ignorance of British beer at the moment. I smiled at the waitress as she noted down our orders. "Hello. I've met you before, but I don't think I introduced myself then. I'm Vivienne."

"Ah yes, of course, the American. I remember you." She smiled back.

"Vivienne, this is Molly. She keeps me supplied with lager on my nights off, for which I'm eternally grateful."

Molly's smile widened. She was clearly fond of Andrew—well, what girl wouldn't be?—but I remembered she had a fiancé, so I did not feel threatened. (Threatened?

What an odd choice of word, really . . . as if I already had a claim staked here, something to lose. Well, I definitely had the latter, if not the former.)

As Molly returned to the bar to get our drinks, Andrew settled into the booth, looking relaxed. He was clearly at home here, but more than that, he seemed a laid-back type of person, the type who could enjoy almost any kind of social situation without undue stress. Maybe he got all his nerves out in the air, flying his plane, and everything he faced on the ground was a breeze by comparison.

We chatted for a few minutes about the weather (not bad these past few days), British sports (I knew nothing about this subject, in any era), and music (he liked jazz, and had in fact played the trumpet when he was young).

"I played the clarinet," I laughed. "And I was a disaster."

"Ah well, that's fine. Not everyone is a musician. I realized pretty quickly I was going to have to find my calling someplace else."

"And would you say you've found it? Flying your plane, I mean?"

"Yes, I guess I would. Though it's not so much about the flying, even though I do love that. I feel like I'm serving my country, helping England in the best way I know how. I feel good about that. It gets me through the tough days."

"I'm happy for you," I said sincerely. Then, I added thoughtfully, "I guess I'm trying to do the same thing in my own life . . . be as much help to the world as I can, in whatever way I can. That's sort of what my new job is about."

"That's excellent, Vivienne. I'd love to hear more about your job sometime if you wouldn't mind telling me."

I nodded. "I'd like that too. Someday, I promise, I'll tell you all about it." Or at least as much as I could. The trouble was, I had no idea where to begin, or how much I could safely divulge, or if he would believe any of it if I told him the whole truth—or run away from me instead. I'd seen enough movies about time travel to know that when the traveler divulges her origins and purpose, the results are generally mixed at best. But I felt, more and more, that I wouldn't be able to lie to Andrew for long.

A few hours later, the bartender was calling time. Andrew paid our bill and thanked Molly, who smiled at us again and wished us a good evening. I stumbled a bit out the door, feeling a head rush from too many lagers and too many swirling thoughts—but for all that, the darkness of Berlin had left me, and I felt, for the moment, really, truly happy.

Moments like that don't often last, but they're always worth remembering.

11

MOLLY

The next few months seemed to pass in a blur as I adapted more and more to life in 1939. I settled into a routine of sorts. When I was in London, I woke early, bought a morning newspaper that I read over breakfast in a coffeeshop near my flat, then headed to the local library to read up on current events. I knew quite a bit about 1939 already, as Gunther had said, but I wanted to get all the details of daily life firmly in mind, learn as much as I could, so that nothing that happened would take me by surprise and so it would seem like I belonged here.

I also kept making trips to Berlin to bring back children to England, fulfilling the terms of my assignment. The trips were all pretty similar to the first one, except that I became less fearful of being caught. I worried for the children, of course—that there might be some glitch with their false papers, that they would start to scream and cry and draw unwanted attention to us at the train station or on the way there. But, fortunately, none of that happened. The operation I was part of—I still wasn't absolutely sure how much was part of the Experiment and how much was being coordinated by people of 1930s Berlin and London with no concrete knowledge of what was to come—seemed to be well run. There were no major missteps, no obvious mistakes, no disasters. Everything seemed to be going according to plan.

As I said, I stopped worrying about being caught, at least in terms of any danger that might befall me if I did. The more I visited Berlin of 1939, the more I felt a strange sense of invulnerability. It felt the way I used to when I was a child and had a nightmare, and then suddenly, my brain woke up enough to remind me that I was only dreaming, that none of what was happening was real. I remembered my childlike sense of confidence, smugness even, as I confronted the monster that haunted my dreams: *You're not real! You can't hurt me! I'm about to wake up and get away from you forever!* It felt like that now. I didn't belong here, so no one in this time had the power to hurt me. For me, this was all like a dream.

(Or so I told myself. Looking back, it's entirely possible I could have gotten hurt in some way, though I'm not sure it would have been possible for me to be killed. Can a person die who hasn't yet been born? I always meant to ask Gunther about this, and every time I started to,

I changed my mind. I preferred to be oblivious to danger and believe in my own invincibility as much as possible. It gave me a reassuring sense of power that I needed to continue doing the things I was doing.)

My lack of fear didn't mean, however, that I enjoyed these visits or was undisturbed by them. I sensed a dark, heavy weight in the air every time I set foot in Nazi Germany. I could feel it in my bones, almost as if it were being absorbed through my skin into my body. Everything was orderly on the surface—the clean streets, the tidy shops, the pretty parks, the people—but I knew what rot lingered beneath. Not that one needed much advance knowledge to be aware of this. The drumbeat towards war was still muted at this point, but it had long since begun and it was obvious to anyone paying attention which way the world was heading. It took a level of willful obtuseness, which I couldn't comprehend but which most of the people around me seemed to have mastered, to think otherwise.

Sometimes, as I walked down the street from the train station on my way to Frau Schroeder's house to pick up the newest arrivals and spirit them across borders to their new life, I paused to look around. Not at the sights and sounds—I'd seen enough Nazi flags and banners to last me a lifetime—but at the people. I couldn't help but wonder who they were, to imagine their stories. Not just up to this point, but in the future. An entire nation had fallen under a madman's spell, and while good people, like Frau Schroeder, were obviously fighting back as in the best way they could, plenty of others were just plodding along, keeping their heads down, waiting for the madness to pass. (I won't even discuss those—and there were many in Germany at that time—who ardently supported Hitler and the things he was doing and promising to do. Historian or not, I've never been able to wrap my head around that part of it.)

Often, I would spot a woman about my age walking down the street, trailed perhaps by a few blonde-haired, blue-eyed children of her own. Mostly, they looked straight ahead, ignoring me, focusing on their destination or their day's errands or whatever was going on inside their heads. I always wondered about these women, about the lives they lived beyond what I could glimpse. Did they support Hitler? Did their husbands? If asked, would they lie and say they agreed with the Führer and his latest actions but secretly hope things would calm down and the worst be averted? Did they believe war would come, and when it finally did, would they survive? In six years' time, this city would be laid waste, and a brutal Soviet occupation would follow. I knew that even those women who survived the war would likely have a rough go of it for many years to come.

And when it was all over, what would they tell their children when they someday learned about the Second World War in school? How would they explain the part they'd played or things they hadn't done? No wonder so many young Germans of the next generation would rebel against their parents, and in some cases turn on them entirely. I probably would have done the same, if I'd found out my mother and father were accountable for enabling a monster who couldn't have risen or held on to power without their nodding acquiescence. I might feel some sympathy for them, but by definition, they were not blameless, because they were here. The stench of guilt was everywhere, and it was almost universal.

These thoughts were futile, of course, and pondering them over and over on every visit accomplished nothing. But I had to do something to distract myself from the sadness of my task and the grimness of the red and black Nazi flags fluttering overhead everywhere I looked.

———————————

Although I often looked at the women my age I passed on the street, I never actually sought one out to speak to. I preferred to observe in silence for a number of reasons, not the least of which was that I knew it would be prudent to interact as little as possible with people in the time I currently inhabited. This was even more true in Germany than in London, where I feared that a word to the wrong person might very well result in real danger to the children I had traveled such a long way to help save.

However, one encounter remains burned in my memory, of a time when a German woman approached me, most unexpectedly, and I got drawn in in spite of myself.

I was walking out of the Berlin train station one morning. My train had arrived earlier than expected, and I had time on my hands and nothing much to do with it. I had no desire to linger in 1939 Berlin—no sensible person would, I thought—but the timing of this trip had made it inevitable that I'd have an hour to kill on the German end.

I decided to use my extra hour as best I could before heading to Frau Schroeder's house to pick up the boy and girl who awaited me there. I bought a newspaper (always good to seize any opportunity to practice my rusty German) and headed to a small café on the corner of the street.

It was quite charming, I had to admit. I'd never spent as much time in Berlin as I had in other German cities, like Munich, but I'd visited a few times during my brief period researching a few years (my years) ago. I'd always enjoyed the *Mitteleuropa* feel of the cafés, with their strong coffee and heavenly-smelling pastries in simulated old-world settings of dark wood and comfy upholstered chairs. The difference was that the cafés I'd visited in the twenty-first century had, for the most part, been recreations, designed mostly for tourists after the country rebuilt from the devastation of the war that was about to begin. But today, I found myself sliding into a leather booth in a café that was undoubtedly the real thing.

I ordered a coffee and an apple strudel and settled in to read my paper. As I mentally struggled to translate the German news articles, I noticed a young couple sitting nearby. They were speaking in low voices, almost murmurs, and I couldn't catch anything that they were saying.

Out of the corner of my eye, I saw the man rise, place some deutsche marks on the counter, and leave the restaurant. The young woman he'd been with remained at the table. I wondered if they'd had a fight, though their conversation hadn't seemed acrimonious. I found myself glancing at her, and trying not to, but something about her piqued my curiosity.

Maybe it was the fact that she kept looking at me.

Normally, in Berlin, I became uncomfortable when anyone looked at me too closely, as if they really saw me. I preferred to float through my assignments like a ghost, an impression from the future who wasn't really there and could easily be ignored. As I've said before, I fit in physically in this time and place, so this normally wasn't an issue. And I did all I could to avoid attracting undue attention.

But this young woman kept glancing up at me. It made me a bit uneasy. So, after a few moments, I finished my coffee, paid my own bill, and walked out of the café, thinking I could spend the rest of the time before my arrival at Frau Schroeder's walking through a nearby park.

A few minutes into my walk, I glanced to my left and saw, to my surprise, that the young woman from the café was right beside me.

"Guten Tag," she said casually, in a lilting accent I couldn't quite place.

"Guten Tag," I replied, caught off guard.

"Are you walking to the park?" she asked, staring straight ahead and not glancing at me.

"Ah . . . yes."

She nodded and kept striding quickly. "As am I. Perhaps we can walk together."

I was startled by the offer and tried to turn to get a better look at her. Blond, green-eyed, pale skin with rosy cheeks. She looked much like every other young German woman I saw walking the streets during my visits to Berlin, but there was a strange intensity about her that both puzzled and intrigued me.

After a few moments of silent walking, we arrived at a bench. This part of the park was secluded, far away from prying eyes (had anyone cared to pry), and out of listening range of strangers. Across the way, an old man read a newspaper, and a middle-aged woman walked a handful of dogs on leads. They were both preoccupied with their own activities, and neither was close enough to overhear the conversation that followed.

"May I ask your name?" the girl inquired as, by silent agreement, we sat down on the bench together.

"Vivienne."

"Ah. Very pretty name. Mine is Helga."

I nodded. "Nice to meet you, Helga." As I looked at her more closely, I saw she was closer to a girl than a woman, perhaps nineteen or twenty at most. Young, I thought, to be on the verge of living through such a dark time in history. I felt instinctively sorry for her; there might be a sense of universal guilt in Berlin these days, but I had a feeling that this girl's only crime had been being born in a time and place over which she had no control. But then, do any of us? With the obvious exceptions, of course.

"Where are you from?"

"America." I responded as vaguely as I could to her question, choosing not to mention my current residence in London. Helga didn't have the look of a spy, but you could never be too careful.

She smiled slightly. "I've always wanted to visit there, since I was a child. It looks so beautiful in the movies. California! Is it really so sunny all the time?"

I smiled. "A lot of the time, yes." My tone became more serious. "How did you know I wasn't German?"

She shook her head. "I heard you give your order in the café. You have an accent, but I wasn't sure what kind."

Damn, I thought. I knew my German was rusty and I was only moderately proficient, but I really should work on ridding myself of my accent and trying to sound more like a local.

"I'm sorry," Helga said, jolting me out of my thoughts. "I must seem crazy to you, asking you all these questions."

"It's all right." I smiled haltingly at her. "Are you from Berlin?"

"A small town a few kilometers away. My husband and I moved here last year, when he was looking for work. And now he's in the army."

I thought of the man I'd seen in the café—actually, now that I thought back on it, little more than a boy himself, probably barely older than Helga. I wondered what fate awaited him in a few months' time, and that made me think of Andrew.

After a moment's silence, Helga leaned toward me, murmuring quietly. "Do you think there is going to be a war?"

I was taken aback by the question and had no idea how I should respond. I grasped for the answer any red-blooded American woman of 1939 would almost certainly give, "I don't know."

She turned away from me, staring straight ahead. I ventured a question. "Do you think there will be?"

Helga paused for a moment, seeming to think before replying. "I don't know either. But—" she kept her eye on the people across the park, though there was no way they could hear what she was saying. "I hope there will be no war. I hope for peace, desperately."

Desperately. I was struck by her choice of words. In the German, *verzweifelt.*

"My father was killed in the last war. I never knew him. I was born just months after he died." Helga looked down at her clasped hands.

"I'm so sorry," I responded, feeling the inadequacy of my words.

She shook her head. "I have four brothers and sisters. My mother raised us all on her own. It was hard for her. And now—if another war comes—my husband is in the army, and so are my three brothers. What will become of them? I worry, night and day. And there is nothing I can do."

She looked straight into my eyes, and I felt the burning intensity of her hopelessness.

I wished I could tell her that perhaps there would be no war. I wished I could be that innocent. But I wasn't, and neither, it was clear, was Helga.

She began to stand, brushing off her skirt. "I hope I haven't bothered you, Vivienne. I'm sure you have many other things to do besides listen to my worries."

Yet she didn't ask me what I was doing there, what brought an American girl to Berlin on the verge of a possible global conflict. I had the feeling she'd simply wanted to talk for a few moments to someone who wasn't from Germany, who didn't belong here. And if ever anyone didn't belong someplace, it was I, right here and now. Somehow, perhaps, she had sensed this.

"I'm glad we could talk." I smiled at her, feeling the sadness she must read behind my eyes. "I wish you the best of luck, whatever the future may hold."

"I wish you the same." She gave me one final, searching look, and bent down to whisper in my ear. "When you return to America, please tell people there that not all of us in Germany want war. Not all of us agree with the things that are happening. I hope that one day, our two nations will be able to be friends."

I clasped her hand and realized I could offer this girl one small piece of reassurance in the middle of all the darkness on the horizon. "I am certain that we will be. One day."

Helga nodded, and before I could say any more, she walked off quickly, disappearing between the trees.

I've never forgotten Helga, or that conversation. I've never stopped wondering what happened to her in the next few years, and the decades that followed. I still wonder if she lived to see the postwar world, the rebuilding, the creation of the United Nations and the European Union to safeguard the peace she had so badly longed for in her youth. Every time I see President Obama and Angela Merkel photographed together at a summit, laughing over some private joke, I hope Helga lived long enough to see the day when history had changed enough that our two nations could finally become friends.

———————————

I was not in Berlin all the time, fortunately. Like any good soldier, I needed my rest periods, and I spent them enjoying London as much as I could.

This meant a regular round of picnics in Green and Hyde parks (as the weather got warmer, and when the periodic bursts of sunshine would allow), museum visits, and even more frequent pub visits. I'd returned to the pub Andrew and I had visited a number of times, sometimes by myself, but often, whenever he was free from his work duties, with him. It was slowly becoming our place—a distinction notable mostly because it meant, bit by bit, that we were becoming an "us."

One day in early June, Andrew was busy flying, and I was mentally preparing for another trip to Berlin the following day. I spent the unusually sunny and warm summer day walking around London, and finally stopped in at the pub for a drink before I was to meet him for dinner back at my place. I'd promised to cook, and he'd nodded solemnly, though I thought I noticed a wry grin when he thought I'd turned away. Whatever he liked about me, he seemed to be aware that domesticity was not my forte.

Since I was alone, I decided to sit at the bar, hoping to see Molly. We'd become rather friendly in the past few weeks as I'd made regular visits to the pub, and I hoped she'd be working today. Sure enough, a few minutes later she came out, smiling warmly, and brought me my regular order.

"Thanks, Molly. Cheers." I raised my glass to her and downed half of it in one go—the heat had made me thirsty. "How have you been?"

"Oh, fine, thanks for asking. It's been busy here lately, but it's a lot calmer today."

"Well, it's still early. And the sun's out, so people are probably enjoying the nice weather while they can."

I had meant this remark casually, but I felt the weight of it after I spoke. *Enjoying the weather while they can.* How many of the people basking in rare English summer sunshine today would be killed in the war that would begin in just a few months' time? The countdown was already on, at least in my head. When I woke up this morning and glanced at my calendar to see that it was June 4, I'd realized with a start that England had less than three months before it would be at war for the next six years.

One of the downsides of traveling to a time that's not your own is that you know everything about the future, and yet nothing. I knew exactly what was going to happen as far as the big picture of the war was concerned, but

I had no idea how it was going to affect individual people. Who would live and who would die? Who would be in the wrong place at the wrong time, and get taken out by a bomb that leveled one side of a city block and left the other side untouched?

It worried me, thinking about Molly—and Andrew. Andrew, an RAF pilot, who in less than three months' time would begin risking his life for his country. I didn't know what would happen to either of them, but the possibilities terrified me.

Attempting to sound casual, I turned the conversation a bit. "So, Molly, do you think you'll be staying in England for a while? Or might you go back to Ireland?"

She looked a bit puzzled by my question, but replied, "Oh, no. Patrick and I are staying here. He's got a good job now, working in a factory a few miles outside London. He couldn't find work in our village back home, no matter how hard he tried."

"I see." Damn it. At least Ireland would have been safe for her and her fiancé; no bombs would be dropping there in a year's time. I wondered how I might subtly convey my concern without alarming her or sounding paranoid and cowardly. "But . . . what if war were to come?" I lowered my voice. There was no one around us anyway, but I felt I shouldn't bring this topic up in a loud voice; it seemed somehow distasteful.

She gazed at me with her bright hazel eyes, her expression quizzical. "Well, hopefully we don't have to worry too much about that. I mean, Mr. Chamberlain made that pact last year, so I figure we should be all right. No one wants a war, do they?"

"No." I sighed and drained the last of my glass. I wished I could tell her to run, to get out while she could before the horrors of the war no one wanted arrived on her doorstep anyway. But there was no way I could tell her what I knew. Even if I were allowed to divulge the future, I would sound crazy if I told her the truth, and she probably wouldn't believe me anyway. Denial is a powerful drug. I couldn't blame her one bit for trusting in Mr. Chamberlain and his Munich Pact. I wished, for a moment, that I was innocent enough to do the same. At least I'd have three more months to enjoy without a sense of dread rising more sharply every day.

I put down my change, leaving her a hefty tip as always, and managed a smile. "I have to go meet Andrew for dinner. Good to see you, Molly."

"Same to you, Vivienne. Come back soon." She smiled brilliantly, the lilt of her Irish accent hanging on the air like song.

I nodded, "I will." I turned to the door and stepped out into the June sunshine, determined to enjoy it while I could.

12

TELLING ANDREW

There comes a time in every relationship where you sense things are getting serious and that it's now or never. If the two of you are going to move forward on an honest and healthy basis, you need to share your deepest, darkest secrets and emotional baggage—whatever those might be—and risk rejection by the other person if it's too much for them to handle. It's never an easy moment.

Of course, for most couples, this conversation does not involve any mention of time travel.

I'd felt the stirrings of guilt about my lies of omission (and outright lies) to Andrew more and more over the past few weeks, as we'd been spending considerable time together, and the conversation had veered more into talking about our pasts. One night a week ago, we'd been at the pub where Molly worked, and she'd come over to join us in conversation at the end of her shift. I'd gained new insight into them both that evening.

"Andrew," Molly asked unexpectedly, after we finished laughing at one of my new boyfriend's jokes about flying and the mishaps he'd experienced during training several years ago, "What made you decide to become a pilot?"

I took a sip of my drink, curious to hear the answer. He'd given me his reasons during our initial meeting several months ago, but I was wondering if, now that we knew one another better, he might share more.

Andrew looked into the depths of his pint glass, as though thinking about his answer carefully. "I've always wanted to fly," he said at last. "Ever since I was a child and first saw a plane in the sky. I thought to myself, how incredible to float so high above the earth! It seemed like magic, like being a bird and having the freedom to leave the ground any time I wanted. But I didn't think it would ever be possible for me, so I did what I thought I was supposed to do—I went to university, got a degree, became a teacher. And that was fine, for a while. But I couldn't shake the feeling that there was something else I was really supposed to be doing."

I nodded soberly; I could certainly relate to that feeling. Glancing over at Molly, I saw that she was studying Andrew intently, her eyes fixed on his, and I wondered if what he was saying resonated with her in some way as well.

"Then a few years ago, one of my university professors wrote to me. He told me that the RAF was looking for young men from Oxford and Cambridge who had a passion for flying and would be interested in enlisting in the air force for training. It felt like a dream, almost like the perfect opportunity landing in my lap. I knew I'd never forgive myself if I didn't take it. So, I said yes, and here I am." He smiled and knocked back the last of his pint in one go.

"Do you ever miss teaching?" I asked him.

"Sometimes, yes. It used a different part of my brain than flying does, that's for certain. I think some day, when I'm a bit older and it gets harder to get in and out of a cockpit, I'll likely find my way back to it. There's more than one job we can have in a lifetime, after all."

I nodded in agreement. Molly, who'd been listening silently as Andrew spoke, now asked another question. "Are you ever afraid?"

"Not really, not when I'm up in the sky. It's hard to explain, but once you reach a certain height it's like all your fears sort of drop away, and you can't remember ever feeling scared. Flying has become natural to me, like anything else if you do it long enough, I suppose."

Molly nodded as if this made sense to her. "You get used to the way your life is. And after a while, you don't really question it much, do you? It all just seems . . . inevitable."

I glanced at her, a bit surprised by her take on Andrew's words, but then I turned back to him with another question.

"So, you're not afraid of flying itself. But what about—I mean, what if someday you have to fight? If war comes," (I forced myself to say *if* rather than *when*) "and you're one of a handful of pilots defending England from danger? Doesn't *that* scare you?"

I felt my words almost as a plea. A part of me wanted him to be scared. I wanted him never to forget the danger of what he was doing, so that he'd never let his guard down, never stop thinking about what could happen to him, and do all he could to stay safe. Or was defending his country from the threat of invasion simply incompatible with self-preservation? Was wanting him to stay safe too much to ask, given the path he'd already chosen, risks be damned?

Andrew smiled at me, as if he could sense some of my thoughts, even though, of course, he couldn't know what I knew about the dangers that awaited him.

"Vivienne, at the end of the day, we're only here for a short while. Life always has an end date. I don't know exactly what the future holds, but if there's ever a time when I'm called on to fight for my country, I'll do it. I'll take the risks, do the job I've signed up to do, and hope for the best. I've realized these past few years that nothing is certain, the future is never guaranteed to anyone, so we might as well just live our lives as best we can here and now. And if I were to go out fighting to protect England, I can think of plenty of worse ends for myself. Don't you agree?"

I nodded slowly. I wanted to disagree with him, but the way he laid out his argument, there was no way that I could. He was right.

These hero types, I thought to myself, sighing. *What can you do with them?*

Then, mercifully, it was last call, and Andrew and I said good night to Molly as we left the pub, and I tried to leave these thoughts behind and do my best to enjoy the moments we had together, right now, before the future inevitably arrived.

It was the middle of August, not long after the conversation in the pub with Molly, when I decided Andrew and I had reached the point in our relationship where I had no choice but to tell him the truth. It was not an easy decision. For one thing, of course, it was a clear violation of the rules of the implicit contract I'd agreed to in coming back to 1939. I could hear Gunther's voice ringing in my ears, instructing me to *tell no one*. And, really, his disembodied voice wasn't wrong. Not revealing your true identity is the first rule for time travelers in any science fiction book or movie, for good reason—and also the most frequently broken. But now, I could understand why. The fact that you are essentially a phantom from the future, a person from another era who won't be born for several more decades, is a pretty lonely secret to keep from the world, and especially from someone you love.

And by this point, I was sure I loved Andrew. I knew it with a certainty born of feelings I'd never felt before in my life that threatened to overwhelm all my idealistic principles and common sense. I knew I shouldn't tell him. I knew it could lead to disaster. And yet, by the middle of August, I'd decided to do it anyway.

I rationalized my decision in several ways. I told myself that, first of all, he probably wouldn't believe me and would end our relationship on grounds of my apparent insanity. But if he did believe me, then I was telling him something he had a right to know. I couldn't continue lying to him, with my vague stories of family in America and a temporary job in London and my desperate attempts to keep up with his 1930s music and film references (that was harder than it may sound; he liked obscure movies). I might be breaking the rules of the game as they'd been set out for me, but this felt more important than honoring an abstract principle. Andrew was a good man; probably the best I'd ever known. He had a right to know the truth before things between us went any further, especially as the time ticked away every single day on my allotted time in his world.

And even if he did believe me, he'd never tell. I was certain of that. It's how I justified my decision, in the end. A secret told to only one person who you believe will take it to their grave is hardly a promise broken, is it? It is. But only just barely.

In any case, that's what I told myself as I sat in my flat waiting for him to arrive for dinner on the night of August 16. It was now one week before the Molotov-Ribbentrop pact between Nazi Germany and Stalin's USSR would be sprung on the world, and roughly two weeks before Germany would invade Poland and kick off World War II. Our idyllic pre-war summer was coming to an end, and the truth needed to be revealed now. I couldn't put it off any longer.

Andrew rapped on the door with three quick knocks, and I let him in. Once he was inside the door, he pulled me into his arms, smiled, and said, "Hi."

"Hi." I smiled back at him, my stomach already twisting in knots in anticipation of the scene ahead. He kissed me, and for a few blissful moments I managed to forget who I was, where I was, and why it was all going to end so soon. Much too quickly, he released me and walked towards the kitchen.

"Ah, bugger, it's been a long day. I'm starving. Want me to cook something for us?" He must have noticed the lack of dinner aromas in my tiny flat, even though I'd said I'd cook, and figured that taking action himself rather than waiting for me to attempt a meal was the best solution.

"Actually, Andrew, I was wondering if we could talk before dinner. There's something important I need to tell you."

"Of course. What's going on?"

"Well, the thing is—it's—you might want to sit down for this." He looked puzzled but did as I asked.

I took a deep breath and, in as few words as possible, told him my story. Everything I've told you here—well, at least the gist of it. It was the hardest thing I'd ever done.

When I finished, I stared at the floor for several seconds that felt like an eternity. I couldn't bear to look up, to see what I feared I would see in his eyes. To sense that things between us—if there still was an "us"—would never be the same again.

Finally, I forced myself to glance up. Andrew's expression, which had gone from curious to dubious to shocked over the course of the last five minutes, seemed to have settled on stony. He wasn't looking at me but staring straight ahead. Maybe he was trying to take it all in, to decide the best course of action before speaking too quickly.

His next words didn't shock me; they were what I had expected. "This can't be true, Vivienne."

He didn't look at me as he said it, but continued staring straight ahead, as if through me, as if I wasn't there. Which in one sense was the truth.

"It's true, Andrew. I know it must be a shock—and I don't know how I'd feel if someone told all this to me. I don't know what I'd believe. I understand if you're skeptical . . ."

"Skeptical?" The word seemed to galvanize him, and he finally looked at me, his eyes filled with a mixture of bewilderment and despair. "You've just told me—you're saying that you are a—that you've traveled back in time, from the next century, to try to . . ." He shook his head, unable to finish the sentence. I couldn't blame him. It had been almost impossible for me to finish, and I knew it was all true.

"I know it sounds insane, Andrew. Believe me, if anyone had told me what I've just told you, I'd have had all the same doubts. It sounds crazy, I know. But it's the truth. I was born on December 27, 1980, which means I won't exist for another forty-one years. I shouldn't be here at all. But I was sent back as part of an experiment that's trying to fix some of the worst parts of the twentieth century. . . ."

I stopped talking. It had been hard enough to say it once. Repeating it didn't make it sound any more believable.

"No. It can't be true." He was looking down again, shaking his head fiercely.

I took a deep breath. "Look, Andrew. There are only three possibilities here. Either I'm lying to you, I'm insane, or I'm telling the truth. You know me well enough to know which of those possibilities is the most likely."

He looked up again, with anguish in his eyes. I knew he was flirting with possibilities two and three and trying to decide which was most plausible. I'm not sure which of them he was actually hoping to be true. Number two meant losing me, and number three meant losing his own sense of reality. Which would he sacrifice?

A moment later, I had my answer. Without looking at me, he got up and walked toward the door.

"September 1st," I blurted out before I could stop myself.

He turned, hand on the doorknob. "What did you say?"

"September 1st. Two weeks from now. Germany will invade Poland and two days later, England and France will declare war. That's how it begins."

He shook his head, opening the door to leave.

"You'll see," I called to the door as it closed (not quite slammed—he was a gentleman, after all) and left me alone in the tiny flat that had never felt more empty. I sank down in the chair Andrew had vacated, exhausted and drained, too tired even for tears.

13

THE WAR BEGINS

September 1, 1939

For all historians, there are certain dates that stand out among others. For a historian of the Second World War, they don't come any bigger or bolder than September 1, 1939. That was the day the world crossed a line it would never be able to retreat from. A day that would change the lives of an entire generation of people forever.

I'd been dreading this day ever since I arrived in London in April. Knowing what was coming and not being able to do anything to stop it was dreadful. But now, ironically, this dark day in history also contained, for me, a kernel of hope.

Andrew.

However, despite the earth-shaking news of the German invasion, any reconciliation or even acknowledgment I'd been hoping for from him failed to materialize. I spent the day alone, holed up in my apartment listening to the news bulletins on the radio, wishing I were somewhere else. Wondering what the hell I was doing here at all.

Aside from the world-historic news on the radio, it was a completely unremarkable day.

September 3, 1939 (two days later)

But here's the thing: never give up hope. Life may not unfold on quite the timeline you're expecting, but that doesn't mean things won't work out eventually.

As it turned out, September 3 was a momentous day in both world history and my own life. England and France declared war on Germany, kicking off the global conflict I'd been studying since I was ten years old. And I received two visitors. One was welcome, the other less so. But both of their visits were important and worth recording.

"For the second time in the lives of most of us, we are at war."

I was sitting in my tiny living room listening to the radio as King George VI—or as he would always be in my mind, Queen Elizabeth's dad—made this solemn announcement to the nation.

That was it. No more uncertainty. No more room for optimism or hope, or faith in the piece of paper Neville Chamberlain had proudly waved to the world a mere one year ago. The game was on; the die was cast. The only question left was who would make it out alive, and who would not be so lucky.

The speech ended. I flicked off my radio, not sure what to do next. I thought of going out, walking to the pub perhaps to see Molly, if she was working tonight, to find out how she was handling the events of the past few days. But even as I reached for my coat, I heard a knocking on my door.

I swung it opened and saw Andrew, in his RAF uniform, looking solemn, contrite, and more handsome than I'd ever seen him. (Did the war give him that extra sheen? Or was I just so grateful to see him again that my own eyes added it like an extra filter? I don't know.)

"May I come in?" I nodded and opened the door wider. He walked in, sat down on my couch, stared at the carpet for a moment and then looked up at me.

"You were right."

"Yes." I'd never been less happy at such an acknowledgment.

"How did you know?"

"I told you how, Andrew." I sat down across from him, staring into his eyes. Determined not to blink. I had to convince him I was telling the truth, to make him believe me. I'd never felt so lonely or adrift. For the past few months, Andrew had been my anchor to this new world, this new time I'd been dropped into. Without him, I didn't know if I could keep my sanity.

He nodded slowly. "I'm sorry—" He broke off, paused for a moment. He looked as if he were rethinking not the apology but what exactly he should be apologizing for. "I'm sorry I doubted you, Vivienne."

I felt a sigh of relief escape me, and I slouched back in my seat. "You don't need to apologize, Andrew. I get it. What I told you was absolutely unbelievable, but it's also the truth."

"So, what you said last time we talked, you're—" He paused again, struggling to bring the words out when he knew how crazy they would sound, whether coming from him or from me.

I spared him the trouble. "From the future. The twenty-first century. 2009, to be exact."

He shook his head. "How can that be?"

I launched into an explanation of the Experiment, as best as I could convey it with my limited knowledge. He stared straight at me while I talked, not interrupting. I took that as encouraging.

When I was done, Andrew shook his head. "I still can't—I can't quite wrap my head around all this, Vivienne. Part of me still doesn't know if I believe what you're saying—if I can believe it. But, I know you. Even if it's just been a few months, I know you well enough to know you wouldn't lie to me about something like this. Or about anything, really."

I nodded. "And you don't think I'm crazy either?"

He smiled, just a slight glimmer, but enough. "No. You seem quite sane to me."

"Good." That was a relief. Even I'd wondered about that a few times.

"So. I guess we've established a few things. You're not crazy, you're telling the truth, you're from the future, and as of today, England is at war."

I nodded. "A good summary, I'd say."

He smiled, but the smile quickly faded. "Vivienne, I—I don't know how to feel about all of this. Not just you and not just us, but today . . . all that's happened these past few days. I don't know what the future holds for me now. I've been waiting for this, expecting it really, but now that it's here, I'm not sure how things will turn out, for me or for the country. And it's terrifying."

I nodded. "I can imagine." But imagine was all I could do, because I knew the end of the story in great detail. I knew the things he did not. How much should I tell him? How much was it safe for him to know? So many questions swirled in my brain that I didn't feel I had the capacity to answer now.

Andrew came over to my chair, sat beside me, and looked earnestly up into my face. "Can you forgive me for not believing you?"

I smiled. "Of course."

He pulled me up out of the chair and into his arms. I remained in his embrace for several minutes, breathing him in, letting my mind stop thinking. Letting go.

After a moment the spell broke, and he was standing next to me holding out my coat. "Come on. Let's go to the pub. I'm due to report in at seven o'clock tonight, but before then, I need one last drink."

"So do I." I took his hand in mine, squeezing it as tightly as I could, and we headed out the door together.

———————————

My next visitor came later in the day and was far less welcome.

Gunther showed up on my door, a few hours after I'd returned home and Andrew had gone into work to begin the official phase of the war, now that it was no longer hypothetical. I should have figured Gunther would arrive to attend to his work in that regard as well.

After briefly inquiring how I was doing and responding to the not-shocking-to-either-of-us news of the past week, he abruptly came to the reason for his visit.

"It's time for you to go home."

He stated it bluntly, without rancor or emotion. It was just a fact.

I'd known this was coming, of course—it had always been the deal—but that didn't make it any less painful to hear his words. Five months had changed a lot. Things were very different now than they had been on the day we met last April—at least, they were for me.

I half-listened to Gunther's plans to return me to the present day immediately, where I would debrief on my assignment and my work would be studied to see what, if any, measurable changes in the course of history had occurred as a result. Before he was more than a few sentences in, I interrupted.

"I'm not going back."

Four simple words. Yet mere words can change the course of history. If they're the right ones.

I expected surprise, outrage, a rush of argument, even threats from him, but instead Gunther stared at me coldly for a moment, then shook his head in disgust.

"I knew this would happen. This is exactly why I didn't want to select you for the Experiment, Vivienne. I was overruled, told that your knowledge would be invaluable and that your passion was an asset, but I had my doubts about you all along."

"Why is that?"

"Because you're a young girl. Your sort is inherently flighty and easily distracted. You've got more grit and determination than many women your age—I'll give you that—but you also have an adolescent idea of romance and an unfortunate propensity for falling in love." He shook his head, bemoaning my simplicity. Clearly, he had been keeping closer tabs on me and my social life than I had realized over the past few months.

"You'd throw everything away for one handsome young RAF pilot? A man who, by all rights, you shouldn't even have met, and whose life was set on a course long ago that doesn't include you? You are a visitor to this time, Vivienne, nothing more. This is not your country, and this is not your home. You were sent here to do a job, and now it's time to go back."

He spoke with finality; there was no room for argument. As angry as I was at his casual sexism and dismissiveness of me in particular and women my age in general, I knew he had a point. I wasn't supposed to be here, in 1939, in

London, in Andrew's life. I'd done what I was sent back to do, to the best of my ability, and now I should gracefully accept the end and move on.

But I couldn't. Not yet.

"This isn't about Andrew," I said as calmly as I could. It was a lie, but the truth at the same time. I couldn't deny I wanted to stay here because of him, but that wasn't the only reason for my stubborn refusal to follow the rules.

"I can't leave now. The war is beginning. It's exactly the reason I should stay! I know things; I can help. I can save lives, protect people from danger—" I paused, thinking of Andrew, Molly, and all those people throughout the city who would soon be hiding in bomb shelters night after night, seeking refuge from the horrors above. "At least, I can try. And I have to. I won't go back just yet. I won't stay forever, but give me a little more time, please."

He shook his head. "Your assignment is over. You must return to your own time. These are the rules of our project. No exceptions can be made."

"Surely some have." I couldn't believe I was the only person who'd refused to return. It was simply impossible to walk away from a world on fire rather than try to help if you were the sort of person who had voluntarily chosen to enter that fiery world in the first place.

He shook his head again. "A few people have remained behind, yes. And many of them have met unfortunate ends. But I am telling you now, Vivienne—go back. It's my best advice to you. If you stay, you cannot foresee the damage you may do. And there is no guarantee you will make it out alive. And even if you do, if you stay and survive six years of war, then what? Do you assume we'll just send you back whenever you please, to your starting point? We aren't a taxi service. This is your arranged day of departure. You must return now."

I shook my head. "Give me another year. A few more months. Let me stay until the war is at a point where I feel I can walk away, knowing I've done everything I can."

"And when will that be?"

I was silent. I didn't know.

Gunther stood up, his gaze fixed on mine. "As I told you when you accepted this offer, Vivienne, you do this of your own free will. You're not a slave; I can't make you return if you don't choose to. But understand that from this point on, you are outside the protection of our program. You must find your own way and navigate this world yourself. We can no longer help you."

I nodded my understanding. "That's fair."

"Fair." He grimaced and stood up. "You are a reckless young woman, Vivienne. I cannot say I am surprised by any of this, but I am disappointed. I had hoped the last few months might have impressed on you the seriousness of the work you were sent here to do. This is not a game."

"That's exactly why I need to stay. For a little bit longer, anyway."

I held his gaze unblinkingly until finally, he broke it, turned away, and shut my door behind him.

I was on my own now. I don't know if I was more exhilarated or terrified, but there was no time to look back. What was done was done, and now I needed to sort out the pieces.

For me, as for everyone else, the war had finally begun.

PART TWO

14

ENGLAND AT WAR

September 1940

T he bombs had not yet begun to fall, but we all knew it was coming.

Everyone knew, not just me. My foresight was unique only in the *way* I knew what every person in England knew right now, in their bones. The war was coming for us, and it would be here soon. Of that, no one had any doubt.

The people around me dealt with this impending fate by plodding stolidly ahead with their daily lives, their outward calm belying the combination of grim determination and fear I imagined they must all be feeling inside. London in the run-up to the Blitz felt like a place where everyone knew what the future would hold, but no one wanted to talk about it. No one was in denial; it was just that talking would do no good. Expressing fear, weakness of any sort, with the enemy coming towards us, possibly any day, could be fatal. So, we all did our best to keep living our lives, day by day, until we finally reached the day in history when the firestorm would begin to explode in the London sky.

Keep calm and carry on. In my era, that was a nostalgic slogan sold on souvenirs throughout Great Britain. In 1940, it was a daily reality—a way of life for us all.

I've skipped over quite a bit in my story, I realize. What had happened in the year since I last recorded my experiences living through the Second World War? Some things you will know, if you are a student of history:

- At the end of September 1939, Poland—after heroically resisting for a few weeks with little to no help from the outside world—fell to Nazi Germany. In accordance with the Molotov-Ribbentrop pact between Germany and the Soviet Union, the Russians rolled into Poland and claimed half of that besieged country for themselves.

- In late 1939, Russia decided to invade Finland. (That didn't go too well.)

- In April 1940, the so-called "phony war" period ended with Germany's invasion of Norway.

- In May 1940, France was invaded and fell to the Germans, leaving the British to fight the war alone.

- In June 1940, the British barely pulled off the "Miracle of Dunkirk," rescuing most of their army from France and ferrying them back to England across the choppy English Channel.

- In the summer of 1940, the Battle of Britain—England versus Germany in the skies, with the fate of mankind hanging in the balance—began.

It was the last point that most concerned me, not as a historian, or even as someone living in England and facing the threat of a Nazi invasion, but as a woman who was completely, utterly, hopelessly in love with an RAF pilot.

(Although *hopeless* is probably not the right word. My love for Andrew, which was in full blossom by the summer of 1940, made me feel many things, but hopeless was not one of them. Indeed, my belief in him—in us—was often all that kept me going. But that didn't mean I wasn't afraid for him every time he climbed into his cockpit in his effort literally to save the world.)

And yet in another way, I did feel hopeless where Andrew was concerned, because I didn't know what would happen to him. That terrified me. And there was absolutely nothing I could do to change it. I was stuck living with the same uncertainty that anyone else alive right now faced who was sending a loved one off to war.

My knowledge of the past (or for everyone else around me, the future, though it was becoming the present every single day) didn't give me any insight into Andrew's personal fate. Would he make it through the war? Would he live to be an old man, regaling children and grandchildren with the stories of his daring wartime heroics? Or would his plane fall from the sky one day, leaving him as just another glory boy cut down in his prime, fodder for romance novelists and movie scripts in the distant, safe, postwar future—the very future he himself had died to make safe? I didn't know, and neither did he.

So, we plodded on every day, steely and determined, doing the best we could to stay hopeful. To believe everything would turn out right. To believe in a future together we both so desperately hoped we would have when all this was over.

When times are hard, people say, turn to your faith. Assuming, that is, that you have any to begin with.

I've always had a bit of a complicated relationship with religion, and with the notion of God. My parents are different religions—Mom is Catholic, Dad Episcopalian—but neither of them terribly devout, or at least not in the regular, church-going sense. Perhaps that's why my sense of religiosity has never been very deeply grounded.

Growing up, I did go to Catholic church with my mother, and she had me baptized so I'd have some form of religion to turn to, I suppose, when times got tough. They were certainly tough now. And a part of me felt that now, if ever, might be a good time to turn to God, or at least the comfort of organized religion. I'm not totally sure what I believe when it comes to the universe or the afterlife or why we're all here, but I do appreciate the value of ritual. As a kid, I'd never let my mom get away with reading me a story without getting every single word right, in the proper order. Every Christmas and birthday, I liked for the traditions to be followed and the presents opened by our family in a specific pattern. Once I find a combination that I like, I eat the same breakfast almost every day for months on end. You get the idea. Ritual and routine, whatever may lie behind them, have always soothed me.

I guess that's why, one sunny autumn afternoon when Andrew was flying, I decided to stop into the small church I regularly passed a few streets away from my flat. It had been a long time since I'd been in any church. I opened the door and was surprised by its weight, and then by the cool air that greeted me inside with its aroma of incense. It brought back memories of being a little girl, holding my mom's hand as we walked into church together. Usually, it was for a holiday service, Christmas or Easter (we were far from weekly mass attendees. My mom's dedication to my religious education apparently had its limits). Perhaps that's why I always associated church services with tedium, something I had to wait through before I could get to the really fun part of the day, like opening Christmas gifts around the tree once we got back home. Church was not my favorite type of ritual.

But, I reasoned, it might not be a bad idea to set about improving my relationship with God, given that the man I loved was risking his life on a daily basis in an apocalyptic battle against evil. I was struggling to remain calm in the face of my fear for Andrew and hoped that, maybe, there was something here that would help me to do so. And if I proved myself worthy, maybe God would be more inclined to listen to my frantic prayers.

I slipped into a back pew, unnoticed by the rest of the congregation. A service was just beginning. The church was a Protestant one—I hadn't noticed the denomination when I entered, but probably Anglican. Church of England. I felt like I was in the right place in at least that sense.

As the reverend intoned words about God, mercy, and forgiveness, I found my mind wandering, as it tends to do in churches. I tried to reconcile these soothing, peaceful words, and the apparent piety of the men and women around me, with the darkness of the world outside these doors.

Darkness, suffering, war, death. None of these were new. I'd studied enough of history's darker moments to know that humankind had been through plenty of nightmarish times before. But still. Knowing what I knew about the atrocities to come, about how many people—many of them young men and women just like Andrew and Molly—were going to be killed in the next few years because of the actions of a cabal of monsters made it hard to feel any sense of comfort from the rituals being carried out around me. Sermons, songs, and prayer were all well and good. Faith certainly had its place in life for many people. I didn't object to any of that; I could even under-stand the need for it, in a way. But at the moment, it all felt so hollow, so much smaller than the nightmare that was unfolding around the globe.

And where exactly was God in all of this, anyway? Mil-lions of people were on the brink of death. If He did indeed exist, maybe now might be a good time for Him to show Himself and put a stop to all of the madness before that happened. I'd joined the Experiment to do just that, in whatever small ways I could. If there was a being out there who actually had the power to stop it all, why exactly wasn't He turning up for duty when the world needed Him most?

As I thought about all of this, I grew more and more unsettled and felt the particular kind of anger rising to the surface that injustice always brought up in me. *I shouldn't have come here,* I thought to myself. It had been a foolish idea, prompted not by any real desire to rekindle what faith I might ever have had, but rather, as an act of desperation. Clearly, the peace and salvation I'd been seeking were not to be found inside this building. At least, not today.

As I shook myself out of my reverie, I noticed that I was now almost alone in the church; the service had ended, and most of the parishioners had left while I'd been think-ing my gloomy thoughts. I began to stand up to leave my seat in the pew, when a deep, soft voice stopped me. "Can I help you, ma'am?"

I turned to see a young reverend, the same one who'd given the service during which I'd just spaced out, smiling at me. His eyes were light blue, his hair was going bald on top, and his smile was very kind. I couldn't help smiling back, despite my gloomy frame of mind.

"No, I'm sorry. I was just getting ready to leave."

"Ah. I hope you enjoyed the service?"

Lying to a man of God was surely a sin at some level, but politeness to kind-looking strangers was ingrained deeply in my own value system. "Yes, it was very good. Thank you."

He nodded. "I don't believe I've seen you here before. Are you new to the neighborhood?"

"Ah, yes. Fairly new. But I don't go to this church—I'm actually Catholic," I said, by way of explanation.

"That's fine. All are welcome here." He smiled again. "If I may ask, what brought you into our church today?"

I sighed, shaking my head. "I'm afraid that's a long story, Father."

He laughed. "That's okay. We're in the long-story business here, as you may have noticed."

I couldn't help chuckling, and suddenly, I found myself longing to confide in this man of God—at least, about some things. I nodded and sat back down in the pew, and he took a seat in the row in front of me.

"I apologize for not introducing myself. I'm Father Smith."

"I'm Vivienne. Vivienne Riley."

He nodded. "Very pleased to meet you, Vivienne." He fell silent, apparently waiting for me to say more.

"I came here today because—I guess I'm struggling a bit these days."

"With what?"

"It's hard to explain." Or at least, hard to say out loud to this man within the walls of his church. It's not as though I could confide my entire story to him, even if I'd wanted to do so. And it felt wrong to say that I was simply feeling the effects of the war for, after all, I was healthy, had a house to live in that hadn't been bombed, and hadn't lost a loved one—at least, not yet. In the land of keep-calm-and-carry-on, what did I really have to complain about?

I went for the simplest explanation. "I'm worried about someone I love. What may become of him."

The reverend nodded, waiting for me to say more.

"My boyfriend is an RAF pilot. As you can imagine, that's about the most dangerous job he could have right now." I paused, and I could feel the tears well up in my eyes. "I worry about him constantly. About what might happen to him."

Father Smith touched my hand gently, nodding with understanding. "I'm sure you do. This is a difficult time for anyone whose loved ones are in harm's way."

I nodded, determined not to let my tears spill.

"Yes, of course. But I'm beginning to realize that it's more than worry, Father Smith. I'm feeling other things as well."

"What sorts of other things?"

I hesitated, unsure how much I should share about my feelings, or even whether it was appropriate to do so. But I was here, in church. I'd come this far looking for answers or peace. If I couldn't find one, maybe I could at least make some progress toward the other.

"The truth is—this war has me questioning everything. Everything I ever believed or wanted to believe."

"Do you mean you're having a crisis of faith?"

I wanted to laugh, for I was pretty sure my faith would need to have been much stronger in the first place for my current lack to be described as a crisis. But instead, I shook my head.

"I'm not sure that's it exactly. I've always struggled a bit about what I believe, to be honest. I hope that doesn't upset you to hear?" I looked at him anxiously, but he merely smiled and shook his head. I suspected he'd heard much worse before.

"I think this is less about losing faith and more about feeling . . . angry."

"Angry at whom?"

"At everyone." The words burst forth from me in a flood, suddenly. "At the men who are responsible for this war, for the state that the world is in. For the unforgivable self-ishness and stupidity of those people who began the last war, which helped lead to the one we're fighting now. At the Luftwaffe pilot in Germany who might shoot down my boyfriend's plane the next time he flies over England to defend the country. They're both doing their jobs, but only one of them is likely to make it out alive each time, and . . . what happens if it isn't Andrew?"

I began to sob, as quietly as I could, though the church was almost completely empty now except for Father Smith and me. He sat in silence, letting my tears fall as my shoulders shook, my head bowed over the pew, probably looking to someone across the nave as if I were praying. Devout. At peace. I had never felt less of either.

Maybe I should have stopped there, but I had more to say, and I couldn't dam the tide of words flowing out of me, even if I'd tried.

"And most of all . . . I'm angry at God."

There it was. Probably the most awful words I could have spoken in a church, to a minister, but at that moment I truly didn't care.

"And why do you feel that way, Vivienne?" I'll give Father Smith this: he kept his cool, just calmly asked the question and didn't immediately call me a heretic or threaten to toss me out of his church. If more men of the cloth were like him, perhaps I would have grown up to be a more regular churchgoer.

I'd stopped sobbing by now, though tears still stung my eyes, so I could speak clearly again. "Because of everything that's happening in the world today. It feels like—like God must have abandoned us. I can't imagine any of this is His will, but why isn't he doing anything about it? Why doesn't he stop evil when he sees it happening? What's the point of being an all-powerful deity who created the universe if you can't help the people living in it when they need you the most?"

I looked up at Father Smith, who was regarding me with a thoughtful expression.

"I wish I had answers to your questions, Vivienne. They are all good ones, and worthy of discussion and reflection."

"So, you don't think I'm terrible for asking them? For feeling how I do?" I didn't think I was terrible—my anger at God, especially in light of what horrors I knew were about to unfold in secret around the world to millions of innocent people—felt justified to me. But I couldn't expect a minister to feel quite the same way.

He shook his head. "No, I certainly don't think you're terrible. And I know you're not alone in feeling as you do. All of us have such doubts sometimes about why the Lord does the things He does, or why things happen the way they do."

"Even you?" I asked him tentatively.

He smiled. "Yes. Even I sometimes question these things. It's only to be expected. We are created in God's image and given minds and free will; it's natural that we should question the world we live in."

"But, in the end, we're still expected to return to God?" Despite everything He's let happen to the world we have no choice but to live in, I wanted to add, but refrained.

"Well, that is the hope. Some people, of course, feel the anger you speak of and cannot overcome it. But as we teach in the Church, God is love. And He created the universe, in all its glory, and created us. By giving mankind free will, He presented us with an enormous gift, I believe: the ability to determine, at least in part, the course of our lives and what we'll do with our time here on earth. But, as you point out, there are men and women who misuse that freedom, and spend their time on earth doing terrible things. This isn't new, as I'm sure you know, Vivienne. Look at history."

Look at history. I had spent my life doing literally nothing else and look where it had gotten me. And as I mulled over Father Smith's words, I realized I'd been given the gift of free will that he spoke of not once, but twice, at least in a sense. First from God, and, then, by the Experiment. I remembered Gunther's words, *"Of course you have a choice. You're not a slave, we can't force you to do anything."* And he was right. I'd chosen to join the Experiment, chosen to come back here to this time and place where some of the worst parts of history had taken place. I'd done it because I wanted to make a difference, and I knew I had: dozens of young German children had been resettled in England, far away from Hitler's reach, in part as a result of my efforts. That was something to remember, a bit of hope to cling to as the world got darker by the day.

But now that my work here in 1940 was essentially done, I realized, I'd lost all sense of control and agency. I no longer felt like an active participant in this world to which I did not truly belong. Instead, I felt like a passenger in the backseat of a car watching the driver careen it over the edge. There was nothing I could do to stop the inevitable crash, and what was the point of raging at God over something that had, in my timeline, happened seven decades ago? It wasn't as if I hadn't known what I was getting into. Maybe I just hadn't been prepared to face the reality of Europe in the 1940s—to experience it not through books and films and academic papers but by living it. Stuck in the same boat with everyone else, only cursed with foreknowledge that made it even harder to bear.

I reflected on all this and realized that the problem wasn't really God, it was me. I had lost my sense of power, my ability to make choices that would make the world better, and that was why I felt so helpless, like I was drowning all the time. I needed to change that. I needed to take my own power back.

"Thank you, Father," I said, finally standing up to leave the pew. "I appreciate your listening to my troubles."

He smiled gently and nodded. "Of course, Vivienne. I hope I've been of some help. And you are always welcome to come back here, any time you like."

I smiled and nodded my thanks, and as I pushed open the door of the church and emerged from the dim light into the surprisingly bright and sunny autumn day, I did feel better. And I had at least the beginning of an idea of what to do next.

Vivienne, the time has come to take a little of your power back and do something good for this wretched world.

And I had an idea of how I might begin to do that—even without the powers of a divinity.

The next day, a sunny afternoon in early September, I stopped by the pub. Andrew was flying again; he had been in the skies for the past week and was due to have his rest from combat soon. I was counting the minutes until he was home, and keeping myself busy in the meantime, as best I could. I'd begun volunteering for the war effort here at home. Because I was relatively unskilled, there wasn't too much I could do that was of great use, but I did what I could. Had there been a way to share my knowledge in any constructive manner, I would have done so in a heartbeat, but I was too afraid. Even though I'd officially severed myself from the Experiment, I wasn't stupid enough to disagree with Gunther's ominous warning about how much damage one could inflict in the present by trying to change it or letting slip knowledge of what was to come. Better to keep my head down. Help in small ways. In fact, since my conversation with Father Smith the day before, I had begun thinking of enrolling in nursing training—despite my strong aversion to blood and the smell of hospitals—since it seemed like a way I could be of service to the war effort without any potential negative repercussions. And it would also be a way of taking back my power to do some good, to fight the darkness in my small corner of the world and stop feeling so gloomy and helpless. After all, Gunther had told me to save lives, however and whenever I could. I'd only be following his orders.

Anyway, that afternoon found me in the pub, and I was happy to see Molly was there too. I wanted to bounce the nursing idea off her, for one thing. Also, any time I saw her, it felt like she brought a bit of normalcy into my life. It was an isolated world I lived in these days—my universe was pretty much limited to myself and Andrew, when he was around, since I was worried about the repercussions of interacting too much with strangers. Still, it was nice to have a friend.

"Hello, Vivienne," she said, coming over to me with a smile and my usual order. "How are things?"

"All right, I suppose. Andrew's on duty today. I'm worried about him."

"Of course, you are." She nodded gravely. "But truly, he's a hero—he and all those other young men. Patrick was just saying to me today he wouldn't be a pilot for any amount of money, and I don't blame him. If I were a man, neither would I. The idea of flying makes me sick, if I'm being honest. I've never done well even with boats. And add in people shooting at you . . ." Molly blushed and looked down at the counter she began vigorously wiping, obviously realizing this train of thought was not comforting to me. "I'm sorry. But please, give him my best, and tell him next time he gets a break to come in here and I'll give him all the lager he wants, no charge." She smiled.

"Thank you," I replied gratefully. "He should be off tomorrow. I'm sure we'll stop by here in the next few days. I know he wants to say hello. He's missed seeing you."

I took a sip of my drink, then said, "Molly, have you ever felt like, I don't know, like you want to do something for the war effort?"

"What do you mean?"

"Well, I've been thinking about becoming a nurse."

She looked at me in surprise, and her eyes grew thoughtful. "Well, that's something. I think you should, if you want to. How does Andrew feel about it?"

"I haven't asked him. You're the first person I've mentioned the idea to."

"Well, I'm sure he'd support you if this is something you want. I think it's a great idea, Vivienne. I wonder what kind of training you need?"

"I'm not sure exactly. My mom was a nurse, and I know it took her a few years to finish school and learn everything she needed to know. But I wonder if there might be ways to speed up the process, because of the war? Surely, they need lots of nurses right now."

"Perhaps." Molly looked thoughtful. She went back to wiping the counter, and we didn't speak for a moment. Finally, she turned back to me with a slight smile on her face.

"Vivienne, if you do decide to do this, can you let me know what you find out? About the training, and what you need to do? I think I might be interested in joining you."

"Of course!" I said happily, delighted at the prospect of having a friend to embark with on this new experience.

"Lovely. I have to go back to work now. But I'll see you and Andrew soon?"

"Yes. We'll be back here in a few days." I paid my check and left the pub.

An innocuous conversation, it would seem. Two young women discussing how they could help the war effort, striving to serve an ideal greater than themselves—at the cost of a lot of blood and toil (especially difficult for those, like myself, with a decided aversion to blood).

It was only later that I would come to see this evening as a turning point. And not for the reasons I might have expected.

15

CAREER GIRLS

As it turned out, Andrew didn't get his anticipated break from flying, because a few days later, the Blitz began.

(Yes, I'd known the dates—the September 7th raid by Germany on London was burned into my memory after two years of writing my dissertation—but I had remained in a bit of denial, still hoping that maybe Andrew would get to take a break before being sent into combat. No such luck.)

The next month or so was a blur. I don't really know how to write about it, even now. Anyway, it's nothing you probably haven't read somewhere else, described by observers far more perceptive and eloquent than I. Suffice it to say, fire rained from the sky for months on end. Buildings crumbled; houses were set ablaze. People began sleeping in underground stations and shelters; it became a normal feature of daily life not to sleep in your own bed. Assuming, that is, that you still had a bed in the morning once Hitler's Luftwaffe pilots had done their worst.

My flat was never hit, fortunately, but that didn't mean I was totally immune from danger. Maybe I did enjoy some special protection due to my odd status as a visitor from the future, but when the air-raid sirens began to ring out their shrill warning on a nightly basis, I didn't feel like taking any chances. I rushed down into the shelters and Underground stations with the rest of London's civilians, hoping to ride out the nightly bombings in safety while being all too aware of the many people who had tried to do the same and been killed anyway.

So, while Andrew was up in the skies, fighting night battles, I was under the earth, seeking refuge from the bombs dropped by the pilots on the other side of this conflict that he was fighting.

I remember one particular night quite clearly. I'd been out shopping for groceries, trying to make the best use of my ration book given my limited cooking skills, when I heard the sirens begin to wail. I immediately ran for the nearest Underground station, which, fortunately, was just across the street. I made it before the bombs began to fall.

That was the good news. The bad news was that the bombs fell all night. This was clearly not a hit-and-run raid; we were past that now. The Germans seemed determined to drop as much fire and explosive material on the city as they possibly could. They'd begun their plan to target civilians, or, put another way, to make the lives of everyday Londoners a living hell until they finally reached their breaking point and waved the white flag of surrender. Not an unreasonable course of action when your city is being set on fire every single night for months on end.

My one sense of reassurance, as I hurried down the steps to begin waiting out the firestorm above, was that I knew that wouldn't happen.

I settled down in a corner of the station, spreading out the blanket I'd brought with me just in case—these days when you left your house, you never knew where you might end up sleeping that evening. I glanced around me. Everyone was quiet, somber. Probably bracing themselves for the next hit that would shake the earth and, if we were unlucky, do enough damage to kill us all. We were laboring under the illusion of safety down here in the depths of the earth, but nothing was certain. No fear could be ruled out as totally irrational. They were all pretty rational these days.

I looked over and caught the eye of a plump-cheeked young woman next to me. She was probably a few years younger than I was. She caught my eyes and smiled wanly. "Frightful night, eh?"

I nodded in agreement. There didn't seem to be much more to say.

She reached over and held out her hand, offering me some of the food she'd brought with her. Clearly, she had come better prepared than I for this evening.

"Thank you," I said gratefully as I accepted the sausage roll she offered. I was famished—I had committed the mortal sin of grocery shopping on an empty stomach and hadn't been able to purchase any food before the sirens began to wail—and devoured it in a few seconds.

"You're welcome. I brought too much anyway." She smiled, revealing crooked teeth on top. I liked her immediately. "I'm Emma, by the way."

"Vivienne." I responded. "Nice to meet you." I grimaced. "Even under these circumstances."

"Yes, it's a bit rubbish, isn't it?" Emma said casually, as if we were in my era, and she was commenting that the DJ in a supposedly hot new London club wasn't actually that good. "Hope this one ends soon."

I nodded in agreement.

Emma continued, whether talking to me or to herself I wasn't really sure. "I sent my daughters out to the countryside a few months ago. Awfully quiet around the house without them."

"I'm sorry," I replied, feeling heartsick. I'd never met the German parents who had entrusted their children to me to smuggle to safety, but Emma's words were a stark reminder that many mothers and fathers here in Britain were doing the same thing. If my own mother hadn't grown up in the countryside, she certainly would have been sent there for safety, too, during the war years. Sent away from her mother at such a young age, to keep her alive so one day she could return home.

War is full of tragedies, both big and small.

"Well, I think I'll try to get a bit of rest," Emma said, arranging her pillow on the cold ground as best as she could. "Nice talking with you, Vivienne."

"You too," I responded. "I hope you get some sleep." *And stay safe.*

That was London in the fall of 1940, in a nutshell. And I must admit, a lifetime of studying that time and place hadn't prepared me to live through the real thing.

———————————

I didn't see Andrew much during those hectic days, though I thought about him constantly. I focused my thoughts on him like a laser beam, whenever I had a few moments free to concentrate, and tried to send him what in my century we would call positive energy. To me, it just felt like desperation, mixed with hope. *Please be all right. Please keep your plane up in the air. Please don't crash or catch on fire. Please don't die.*

I repeated these mantras in my head, over and over. Maybe they worked. Maybe they didn't. Like anyone else alive at that moment, I was just trying to hold on to hope, using it as a weapon and a shield.

However, as endless as my worry about Andrew's safety was, it would be wrong to say it totally absorbed my every waking moment. That honor was reserved for my new vocation: nursing training.

As a child, if you had asked me what I wanted to be when I grew up, nursing would have been pretty far down on the list. My mom was a nurse, and while it was a perfect profession for her—she loves helping people and has no aversion to sickness, hospitals, or awful smells—I did not inherit her strong stomach or generosity of spirit. When I signed up for the Experiment, my major motivation was to help people: to change the past to make a better future. But even that decision, I realized, had not been completely unselfish. A significant part of my willingness to go back in time to one of history's darkest moments was to satisfy my own lifelong curiosity. For a history student, it was the ultimate exercise in academic field work. How could I turn that down?

Nurse training was entirely different. In fact, I think it's safe to say it was the only completely unselfish thing I've ever done in my life. And that really is true, because I hated every single minute of it.

————————————

After my conversation in the pub with Molly, I did some research and discovered that there was indeed an increased need for nurses, given the outbreak of war, and expedited training programs had been created as a result. So, Molly and I signed up together—such a casual decision, looking back on it now, with neither of us realizing how it would end up reshaping our lives.

We arrived at our new hospital one Monday morning at seven o'clock and promptly joined a group of thirty other young women, all of us looking somewhere between glowingly excited and absolutely terrified. We received our uniforms, complete with capes and name badges, and were quickly thrust into the daily routine of life as student nurses.

And it was a routine like nothing I'd ever experienced before. We toiled for up to twelve hours at a time, days and nights, learning how to do everything from scrub a bedpan to bandage a wound to attempt to calm the nerves of our patients while maintaining courteous professional detachment. And when our workdays were over, we had our course of study, in which I learned more about anatomy and the ills that can befall the human body than I ever thought possible.

It was hard, exhausting work, at least for those of us who did not possess the natural attributes of nurses but had plunged into the traineeship anyway, naively determined to do good despite our own limitations. By that, of course, I mean me.

I had begun the program with the best of intentions, but it didn't take me long to realize that good intentions alone were not going to be enough. The more I dove into my work, the more I realized a simple truth: I hated everything to do with nursing and medicine.

I hated the hospital and its odors. I hated scrubbing bedpans. I hated seeing sick and injured patients every day. As much as I wanted to help them, it was all I could do to keep from running out of the room every time I saw an open, gaping wound, which was far more often than I would have liked. Most of all, I hated the sight of blood, which seemed to become more routine every single day.

But I drove on, determined to be worthy of my new assignment. Maybe I couldn't save the world from Hitler, but I could do some good here. I could help people who were suffering, if not in the way I might have chosen. And—here's the part that I guess is a bit selfish—I could justify my decision to defy Gunther and stay in London. I was helping people. I was doing good. *See, Gunther, it wasn't just about the handsome RAF pilot and my stupid propensity for falling in love! I'm doing something of value here that I can't do anywhere else.* That justified everything, as far as I was concerned.

But if I didn't take to nurse training, the same could not be said for Molly. From the first day we showed up together for our training course at Montgomery Hospital in central London, she had been the star of our class. Not that she tried to show off or show anyone up, of course—that wasn't her way. But as it turned out, Molly was really, really good at nursing. She immediately picked up the rhythms and routines, scrubbed bedpans with abandon and no apparent disgust, and conquered our bookwork with the same ferocious zeal. I'd always thought of her as mild-mannered and sweet, but nurse training revealed another side to her: fiercely determined and astonishingly competent, with a bedside manner anyone would want in their time of need. I have to admit I was very impressed with her transformation.

One free Sunday in October, we stopped by the pub (Molly had quit her job there to throw herself into training full-time, with the idea that she'd become a nurse soon and make better money anyway, but they still let her, and now me, drink for free), and while we downed our lagers, I asked Molly how she was enjoying our program.

"It's brilliant, Vivienne," she said, her eyes shining. "Truly, I can't thank you enough for convincing me to join you! It's been the most amazing thing that's ever happened to me."

I couldn't muster her enthusiasm for hospital life, but I was glad to see her so happy.

"Well, you're doing great. You'll make a wonderful nurse. Patrick must be very proud of you."

Some of the light in her eyes dimmed, and she looked down at her drink. "Did I say something wrong?"

"No, not really. It's just . . . we've been rowing a bit about that, to be honest."

I was surprised. "You mean he doesn't want you to become a nurse?"

"It's not that exactly. It's more that he . . ." She paused, and I realized she might feel uncomfortable saying anything negative about Patrick to me, perceiving it as disloyalty. "He wants to get married soon. He's making good money now in the factory, making war materials, and he says the time is right for us. But, Vivienne, I don't know."

Puzzled, I asked, "What don't you know?"

Molly took a deep breath, looking down at the table, then up to meet my eyes. "The truth is, Vivienne, I don't know if I want to get married. To him, or to anyone else."

I sat there for a moment, feeling shocked, and hard upon that, wondering why. I'd known Molly for over a year now, and while I wouldn't have described us as intimate friends exactly—mostly because there was too much I couldn't tell her, or anyone else except Andrew, so I kept her and everyone else at a bit of a distance—I thought I knew her well enough that she couldn't surprise me much. She'd talked about Patrick as long as I'd known her, and I'd always assumed their marriage was not a matter of if, only when.

To hear her speak this way was a revelation, but why? Because I'd assumed she wanted the same life almost every other young girl in England in 1940 wanted—marriage, children, stability? Because I hadn't, perhaps, credited her with even having the imagination to want anything else, or anything more?

I realized Molly might interpret my silence as disapproval, so I spoke up. "Wow. I didn't realize. I thought you two were just waiting for the right time for your wedding. I didn't know you felt this way." I felt guilty for not knowing, like I was a poor excuse for a friend. All this time, Molly had clearly been experiencing some level of dissatisfaction with her life, some emotional turmoil I hadn't picked up on. Granted, I'd had plenty of other things on my mind, but still. It wasn't as if I had such a wide circle of friends in 1940 London that I should neglect the only real one (aside from Andrew) I'd made here. I resolved to do better, starting right now.

"Tell me more, Molly. You can talk to me. What's going on?"

She looked at me with a strange expression on her face. She took a deep breath and spoke, hesitantly at first, but soon the words were pouring out.

"Patrick and I have known one another all our lives. We met as children; his family lived a few houses away from mine, in our village in Ireland. We grew up together. I'm not even sure when we started—I guess you might call it walking out together—but that's not even what it was to us, really. We just started spending more and more time together, and one day, he asked me for my hand. But we knew we couldn't make a go of it at home; we were too poor for a house or a family, and there was no work to be had there. So, we decided to move to London, hoping to find work here."

She shook her head. "I never in a million years thought this would happen, Vivienne. I mean, when you suggested nurse training, I thought it might be interesting, a different way to earn some money and help with the war effort at the same time. But the truth is, I love it. I love work. I love having a career, earning more money, having more independence. Patrick doesn't understand that at all. He wants us to get married now, and then for me to quit my job and stay home and be a housewife. But I'm not sure I can. I'm not sure I'm suited for it anymore, if I ever was. The life I see in front of me now is the one I want. And I don't know how to tell him that!"

I touched Molly's arm and turned her towards me. She looked a bit frightened and embarrassed at having expressed her thoughts this way, but there was also a touch of something else in her gaze—defiance, perhaps. And it made me think of my mother.

───────────────

Mom had left England years ago in her early twenties after completing her nursing training in London. At the age of eighteen, she'd announced to her parents that she was moving from her small village to London, on her own, to become a nurse. Her mother hadn't wanted her to go, for reasons I never completely understood, and it had been the source of some friction between them. Mom was the oldest child in a big Catholic family where a sense of duty ran deep, and adventure was not so much frowned upon as considered altogether impossible. My grandmother hadn't seemed to understand at all why Mom might want to do anything else with her life other than get married, settle down in the village, and have one baby after another. Nevertheless, she'd done it—pulled up stakes from her little English village, traveled around the world as a nurse for years—Australia, South Africa, Kenya, and finally New York, where she'd met my dad. Along the way, she'd had countless adventures, made friends from around the world, and discovered her vocation in helping people heal that she'd continued working at for the rest of her life.

As a child, I'd loved hearing stories about her travels and escapades around the globe. Mom had been a role model for me since I was little, showing me as a young girl and then a young woman that there was nothing in the world I couldn't do, or at least try. But it wasn't until

I became an adult that it really occurred to me how difficult her decision to leave home must have been. I realized, finally, how brave she'd been, and how her courage had blazed a trail for me.

I saw something similar now in Molly's eyes—the same type of determination and stubbornness I imagined Mom must have displayed all those years ago. She was daring to dream of a different life for herself than what the world and the people around her had always told her she could have. I couldn't help being impressed by her courage.

And maybe, I thought, I could help her, be the voice of encouragement, the friend and support system that my own mother never had.

"Listen, Molly. I know exactly what you're saying. I know it may seem like every woman our age wants the same things—marriage, kids, a house—and that's fine, if it's what you want. But it's also fine if you don't. You can want something else, and that's perfectly all right too. I mean, look at me. I haven't exactly followed a conventional path. I spent years in school getting my degree, and I'm planning to eventually teach history at a university"—once I finish changing that history to improve it, I added silently—"and that's what's right for me. That's my dream. You know I love Andrew, but just having a boyfriend, or a husband, wouldn't be enough for me either. I want more. And it's absolutely okay if you do too. In fact, I think it's great!"

I smiled warmly at her and, after a moment's hesitation, she smiled back. She now wore the expression of a drowning person who's been thrown a life preserver.

"Thank you, Vivienne. You don't know—I mean, that means so much to hear you say that. I don't have any other friends who I can talk to about this type of thing, and my family would never understand. And Patrick . . ." She broke off, sighing. "I don't know. I'm not sure what to say to him, but I think you're right. And I think it's time he and I sit down and discuss a few things. Now that I've told you all this, I feel so much better. I feel like I can face him and tell him the truth. I just hope he'll understand and won't hate me for it."

"I'm sure he won't. But no matter what, you're doing what's right for *you* and following your heart. I'm sure you'll never regret it." It was a string of cliché sentences, but I didn't care. If any situation called for a good cliché, I thought, surely it was this one.

Molly smiled at me again in gratitude, and I beamed back. The truth is, I felt great. I was sorry for Patrick, given that he was probably a nice guy who might get hurt through no fault of his own, but I was proud of Molly for deciding to follow her dreams, to claim her own place in the world.

And I was, I'm ashamed to admit, more than a little proud of myself too. Here I was back in 1940, helping a young woman find her voice! I was giving Molly a seventy-year head start on living the life I had always taken for granted. Maybe this night alone was reason enough to justify my presence here. Who could tell?

Looking back now, I felt so insufferably proud and even smug that evening that I'd like to smack myself, hard. But it's easy to feel that way when you know, in the wisdom of hindsight, how a story will end.

That night set something in motion. I knew it. I just didn't know what exactly it was, or what the consequences of Molly's actions—and my own—might be.

"*I'm sure you'll never regret it,*" I told Molly in that pub on a chilly night in fall 1940.

Those words haunt me to this day.

16

THE PLOT THICKENS
(OR IS REVEALED)

I t was a week or so before I saw Molly again. We passed each other here and there in the hospital corridors during our work hours, but we didn't really have time to talk.

By now, we'd completed our initial round of training and were on our way to being full-fledged nurses because of the compressed wartime training schedule. At least, Molly was well on her way. I considered quitting every single day. I had not been able to acquire the knack of cleaning bedpans fast enough for the ward sister's liking, and she let me know this, repeatedly. She was right, of course, but this did not make me feel any better. If ever anyone was more unsuited for a profession than I was for nursing, I don't know who it might be. But I plugged on, telling myself I was helping the war effort, and (if I was honest with myself, late at night before falling asleep) that as long as I continued to do so, I could rationalize remaining in 1940. With Andrew.

Finally, I got a chance to catch up with Molly. It was Saturday, our day off from work, and I'd invited her over for tea. Andrew was flying again, and if I didn't have work to distract me, I thought seeing a friend might help soothe my nerves.

As it turned out, that was not the case.

Molly burst in my door with an excitement I'd never seen from her before, and before I could say a word of welcome, she blurted out, "Vivienne, I have to tell you what's happened!"

"Tell me!" I smiled. It was wonderful to see her so happy. The gentle melancholy that often seemed to haunt her face had lifted like fog, and she looked absolutely lovely. I had never quite realized before just how pretty she was.

She sat down, accepted my cup of tea, and took a deep breath. "Well, I did it. I had a talk with Patrick."

"And?" I leaned toward her eagerly.

"And I told him the truth—that I can't marry him. Not now. Maybe not ever. It just wouldn't feel right. I love my work too much to want to quit, and it wouldn't be fair to him to marry him when my heart wasn't truly with him, you know?"

"Absolutely," I nodded in agreement.

"I told him that, in those very words. He was hurt at first, but . . . here's the thing, Vivienne—I think maybe a tiny part of him was relieved as well. I could be wrong, but I think maybe he's had some doubts about us too. Not because he doesn't love me, but it's like we never really had a chance to make up our own minds about getting married. It was sort of put on us by our families. And now . . . now we can choose our own future. And even if that means not being together, I think in the end it will be worth it."

"I'm sure it will. I think you're absolutely doing the right thing, both of you. Marriage is a serious thing, and if you're not ready, you shouldn't jump in. And you shouldn't have to give up nursing! I've seen how much you love it, how good you are at it. You shouldn't sacrifice that for anyone. It makes you happy, and you're helping so many people. Maybe this is what you were put on earth to do."

"God's plan for me, you mean?" Molly looked thoughtful, holding her mug of tea and staring into the distance. "I never thought of it that way, but you could be right."

We chatted for another half-hour or so, then Molly grabbed her things to leave. Her head must have still been in the clouds a bit, because after I'd walked her to the door and turned back, I noticed she'd left her purse behind. "Don't forget this!" I called out. She dashed back and grabbed it, smiling gratefully.

"Thank you so much, Vivienne. What would I do without you?" And with another quick smile, she was gone.

I walked back into my flat and sat down on the chair she'd just vacated. It was then I noticed something that must have slipped out of her purse. Picking it up off the floor, I saw it was a small photograph of Molly and a young man, who I presumed to be her now ex-fiancé, Patrick.

I glanced at the photo and was about to put it back on the table, making a mental note to bring it to Molly next time I saw her, when something caught my eye. I examined the picture again. Molly and a handsome, dark-haired young man, his armed linked through hers, a smile playing on his face.

Something about the man looked familiar. He reminded me of someone. A ghost of the expression called up a memory I couldn't quite place, but it troubled me for a reason I couldn't articulate. What was it? There was no way I could ever have met Patrick, surely.

I sat thoughtfully for a minute, trying to pinpoint the source of the familiarity of the young man in the photo, but I drew a blank.

Finally, I shrugged, got up, and went to make some tea. My mind wandered to other things, mainly what Andrew and I would do when he got his next break from flying and I had a free day from nurse training. But something nagged in the back of my mind all the while.

I sat down with my tea and picked up the photo again. Suddenly, unbidden, an image of my Uncle Patrick, my mother's brother, popped into my head. That was who this man reminded me of, I realized. Something about the smile. How odd that they had the same name!

How odd. . . .

I put down my tea. My mind seemed to have slowed down, then suddenly, it speeded up exponentially as revelations tumbled over another at breakneck pace.

Patrick O'Toole. That was my uncle's name. O'Toole was my mom's maiden name. Even though she'd been born and raised in England, her parents were immigrants from Ireland.

My grandfather had died several years before I was born. I'd seen photos of him when he was older, and he'd looked pretty much like any old man, nothing that would really stick in one's memory. But I remembered my uncle visiting us in America when I was a child. His smile, his laugh, how infectious it was. I liked him so much I hadn't wanted him to leave. I cried on the day he went back to England, missing his jolly laugh and the way his eyes crinkled up at the corners when he smiled, and spent the next few weeks pestering my mother with questions about when Uncle Patrick would return.

Young Uncle Patrick's face was burned into my memory from that visit, and it looked very, very similar to the face of the man in the photo Molly had left behind.

My grandmother, Margaret O'Toole, had lived to be an old woman, but I'd only met her a few times in my life. We lived far away, and she didn't like to fly. I never really got to know my grandmother; I never even asked her any questions about her life during the war, despite my interest in history. Somehow, it just hadn't occurred to me to do so.

I'd never seen a photo of my young grandmother. I had no idea what Margaret had looked like as a young woman. But there was no mistaking Patrick O'Toole.

Molly's last name wasn't O'Toole, of course. It was Brennan. Because she wasn't married yet.

No. It couldn't be. It wasn't possible. No. No. No. No.

17

THE REVELATION

Y es."

I spoke the word to Andrew, pacing around his flat. I couldn't sit still. My mind had been whirling nonstop since I'd seen the photo of Patrick a few days ago, and I'd been aching for him to return from the skies, even more than usual, because he was the only person I could talk to about what I had discovered. The disaster I had unknowingly set in motion.

"You're saying that Molly . . . that Molly is . . ."

"My grandmother." I plopped down on his couch, shaking my head and squeezing my eyes shut. "Yes."

"But that . . . that's not possible. How can that be? I mean, what are the odds of such a thing—"

"Staggering," I replied. But that was cold comfort. I had too much on my mind to be amazed by statistical probabilities right now.

"But look here—I mean, you could be wrong. Patrick O'Toole—that's a fairly common name in Ireland, surely? There must be loads of them. Maybe there's some way to find out . . ."

I'd never longed for Google and social media more than I had in the past few days. In the time since I'd made my initial discovery, I'd done all I could to confirm my theory, which in the twenty-first century would have been relatively easy. It was more of a task in 1940, but still possible, if you knew whom to talk to and what questions to ask.

I'd begun by grabbing Molly at work two days ago, as we were leaving our shifts. I'd convinced her to go for coffee with me at a café across the street from the hospital. I'd seized the opportunity to carefully prod her with a few innocuous questions.

By the end of our conversation, I'd learned a few new things about Molly and her life. I'd discovered the name of the village she and Patrick had come from in Ireland— the same as the one on my grandmother's birth certificate, which I remembered from the time Mom and I had gone through a box of her things after she'd passed away a few years ago. And I'd confirmed my other suspicion: Molly was a family nickname, not her given name. That was, as I had suspected, Margaret Brennan.

Those facts were damning enough, but there was something more. I remembered the first time I'd met Molly, she'd reminded me of someone, though I hadn't been able to place who. Now I knew. It was something about the eyes, or the mouth, or both—but looking at her now, in light of my recent discovery, I could see my mother in my grandmother's face. She reminded me of old photographs of my mom in her twenties, and even how she'd looked when I was very young, if I scoured my memories hard enough for those images.

So, there it was. Molly—my friend, my confidante, the woman I'd spent the past year and a half getting to know, despite my stern injunction from Gunther not to make friends with anyone from this time and place—was, in fact, my grandmother. She was destined to give birth in less than a year's time to my mother, who in a few decades would have me. Except for the minor detail that I might have screwed all of this up irrevocably with my meddling.

"Andrew, what am I going to do?" I moaned, after I'd explained everything I'd learned in the past few days to corroborate my theory. "I mean, I just told my grand-mother not to marry my grandfather. And she listened to me. And . . . and she seems so *happy* about it. But if they don't get married, my mom will never be born, and I won't—"

I trailed off and shook my head and let it fall into my hands. How had I created such a mess?

"Vivienne." Andrew walked over and wrapped his arms around me, kissing the top of my head. "It's not your fault. You didn't know . . . How could you have?"

How, indeed. He was right, but I had also been wrong, I realized now. Wrong to try to tell Molly what to do with her life when I had no way of foreseeing the consequences. Even if she hadn't eventually become *my* grandmother, chances are she would have been some-one's. In the future, the time I came from, generations of people existed because of the decisions that had been made back in 1940—decisions, I could see now, in which I'd had no right to interfere.

Gunther was right, I thought bitterly. I wasn't cut out for this. I was nothing but a stupid girl, besotted by an RAF pilot, and determined to help her friends find happi-ness. Happiness that, if they succeeded in finding it, could destroy the lives of countless people in the future. And not just any people; people whom I loved. My Uncle Pat-rick, my aunts and cousins. My own mother. And me.

As these thoughts swirled in my head, panic began to set in. I had to fix this mess. But how?

I raised my tear-stained face to Andrew and asked the same question. "How can I fix this? What am I going to do?"

He stroked back my hair and kissed my forehead. "We'll figure it out."

––––––––––––––––

We talked for the rest of the evening, trying to come up with a solution but not finding any. Finally, we went to bed. I was exhausted and wanted nothing more than to fall asleep and hurl myself into oblivion, but I could tell Andrew wanted to talk.

"Vivienne?" he said, as my head hit the pillow and I closed my eyes, hoping for a good long rest.

"Yes?"

"Tell me about the future."

I sighed, rolling over to face him. This was a conversation we'd had a few times before. Andrew was fond of asking me for hints about what the future held. I certainly couldn't blame him. If I were dating someone from seventy years ahead of my own time, I'd have plenty of questions. But I'd always been hesitant to indulge his curiosity. I mean, strictly speaking, he wasn't even supposed to know about the Experiment, who I was, where and when I'd come from. I'd let him in on all of that regardless. No doubt Gunther would be furious if he knew, and not without reason. Perhaps because of guilt over my failure to fully keep the big secret I'd been let in on, I'd guarded other secrets as closely as I could. I felt that the less I said to Andrew about the future, about the things that I knew were coming, the better.

And it wasn't just Gunther's warnings that compelled me. I was worried about telling Andrew too much, for his own sake. Knowing what's coming next in life can be a heavy burden. I'd found that out, to my cost, in the year and a half since living here. Some days I felt physically older, drained, worn out by my awareness of the horrors that were to come, for tens of millions of innocent people. I didn't want to share that with Andrew, to make him feel the sense of foreboding that haunted me as I went about my daily life. Wake up, have breakfast, buy a newspaper, pick up my ration book, think about Auschwitz. Honestly, who wants that kind of information burned into their brains? What good could come of sharing it?

Of course, I could have told him the happy parts too. I could have told him about May 8, 1945, and the British celebrating in the streets of London after Hitler had been defeated at last, and the bombs had mercifully stopped falling. But as I'd learned this past year, there is no happiness without sadness. They are inextricably intertwined. I couldn't tell him how the war would end one day without also revealing how much suffering would happen before then, how the world would grind on under cover of darkness for half a decade before it finally saw the light. And postwar Europe wasn't exactly a picnic either—one day of celebration would be followed by decades of rebuilding, and a hard life for just about everyone.

And aside from all these worries, there was something else that kept me from wanting to share details of the future with Andrew—my fear that he might not be around to see it. I didn't know what would happen to him. I didn't know if he was going to survive the war and live to a ripe old age, or if there was a Luftwaffe pilot falling asleep in Germany right now who was soon destined to shoot him down and end his life. Not knowing was torture for me, and I knew it was hard for Andrew too, but he accepted it as part of the job he'd signed up to do. But it felt somehow cruel to dangle information, either good or bad, about a future he might never live to see.

So, I kept my silence.

That night, however, Andrew was not to be denied. He reached out and touched my cheek, turning my face fully toward his so he could look me in the eye.

"I understand you can't tell me everything. But Vivienne, honestly, there are times when I think about everything that's happening around me and—I hate to say this, but it's true—I almost give up hope. The darker things seem, the more I'm losing my faith that the world will come out of this in one piece. I don't know that we'll ever be able to sort things out and create a decent world again, for our children and grandchildren. And if that's not what I'm fighting for, then what's the point? Why am I putting myself in danger every time I get into my cockpit to fight Germans, if there's no hope for the world left at all?"

I stared at him in astonishment. I'd never heard Andrew talk like this before. He'd always been so steady, so strong, so determined to fight the fight he'd signed up for. I had no idea he'd had these feelings of despair, but I couldn't blame him. I still didn't feel right telling him about the details of what was to come in the next few years . . . but maybe it wouldn't hurt to describe the world of the future, my future, that would eventually rise out of the ashes of the horrible war he had to fight now, day by day.

"Okay," I agreed finally. "I'll tell you about the future. But only about things that will happen decades from now, okay?"

He nodded eagerly, looking at me expectantly.

I thought about the past seventy years of history, from 1940 to my own present, and hardly knew where to begin. So, I decided to paint the happiest picture I could for him.

"Well, first of all, in 2009, Europe will be at peace."

He looked at me intently, his eyes hungry for more. "Truly?"

"Truly. There hasn't been a war between the major European powers in decades. Things are pretty quiet over here—one might even say boring." I smiled slightly.

"Boring?" he laughed. "Somehow I can't picture that."

"It's true. A lot of my friends in college and grad school didn't understand why I wanted to study European politics, when there were so many more interesting parts of the world to focus on—according to them, at least."

"But you choose Europe anyway."

"Yes. It's the part of the world that appealed to me most." I didn't add that the hard-won peace and stability—the "boredom"—was a huge part of that appeal. History is full of harsh chapters, and I've always been a sucker for the rare happy ending.

"So, go on. Europe is at peace, really?"

"Really. England, France, Germany—they're all allies. There's even something called the European Union—what Churchill once envisioned as a 'United States of Europe.' I mean, it's not the same as the US, certainly—twenty-seven countries are members of it, and they have their differences at times—but they don't go to war with one another anymore."

He shook his head in wonder. "Incredible."

I nodded because he was right. It really was incredible. And every time I rushed to take shelter in an underground station these days, fleeing German bombs aimed at the residents of London, I was reminded of this once again.

"Yes, it is. You might say it's a miracle. But I won't lie to you—it takes a long time and a lot of struggles to get to that point. It doesn't come easily. But it will come. I promise you that, Andrew."

He closed his eyes, smiling, and nodded. It seemed this assurance about the future of Europe was enough for him, that I didn't need to say any more. But now that I'd started talking, I didn't want to stop. There was so much more I could tell him. . . . So many things that seemed unimaginable now that would come in the future I so desperately hoped he would survive to see. Maybe by telling him about some of them, I could help him fight even harder to make it through the war, to live to experience the things I was describing.

"Want to hear some more?"

He turned to me with an expression of excitement. "Sure. Go on. What else does the future hold?"

I thought for a moment. "Well, in 1969, a man will walk on the moon."

That made him shoot bolt upright in bed, astounded. "You're kidding!"

"Absolutely not."

"It can't be. You're making that up."

"Why would I make it up?"

"Because you know I can't argue with you! You can tell me anything and I'll have to either believe it or call you a liar. I have no leg to stand on here."

"Andrew, I'm telling you, it's the truth. July of 1969. My parents watched it happen on TV."

"TV?"

Oh, wow, we were going down a rabbit hole now. It was easy to forget just how much of my world was completely foreign to Andrew, even after I'd lived in his television-free era for so long. "Um . . . it's sort of like radio, but you see pictures. Or a movie theater you can keep in your house. It's pretty cool. You'll enjoy it."

"A cinema that fits in your house? Now I've heard everything. England and Germany as allies is nothing compared to that." He grinned.

I smiled, trying to think of what else to tell him about. "Well, if you think that's impressive, what would you say if I told you that one day, in my lifetime, there will be a way to look up any piece of information about the world you could possibly want to know in seconds?"

He frowned. "I'd say that sounds impossible."

I nodded. "I know it sounds crazy, but it's true. You just type in any question you have into this enormous system, and you can get an answer back instantly."

He shook his head. "That's amazing. Anything?"

"Virtually anything. I'll give you an example. Years ago, my dad and I were talking about a political leader from a few decades earlier, and my dad suddenly asked me, 'Is he still alive?' And I realized I didn't know and had no way to find out unless I looked it up—in a book, and even that might be outdated. If you miss the news when something happens, you're out of luck, right? But in the future, this stops being a problem because if you ever wonder about someone's life, or some event in history, or anything that's happening in the present, you can just sit down, type out your question, and you'll get an answer back. Millions of answers, in fact."

Andrew shook his head, looking stunned. I tried to imagine how hard it would be to wrap my head around the concept of the internet if it were completely unfamiliar to me. I remembered a world without it, but when I'd first arrived in 1939 it was hard to recall what it felt like to have to rely on books, newspapers, and my own memory for information. It took a while before I stopped automatically reaching for my iPhone to google any questions I might have.

"Well, that's quite something. I can't begin to imagine how that would change the world—having answers to any question you want at a moment's notice? It must do wonders for education."

I smiled. Clearly, there was a part of Andrew that retained his teacher's mind.

"I'd love to say that's true, but honestly, it's not all good. A lot of misinformation can be more quickly shared as well as facts. That causes a lot of problems. And lots of time, people just use it as a way to chat with their friends and share their opinions. And photos. Everyone's sharing photos instantly with one another, all the time." I laughed. "You don't have to wait days or weeks to get them developed anymore."

He laughed. "I'm not sure that part would really be helpful. Though it would be nice not to have to wait so long to see if a photograph you've taken is any good."

I smiled, trying to think what else to tell him about. Then I remembered I'd left out some of the really important details about the world to come.

"Oh, yeah . . . in 1979, England will have its first female Prime Minister."

His eyes widened. "You're joking."

"No, I'm not. Why . . . do you have a problem with a woman leading your country, Andrew?"

"No, but I can't imagine such a thing. Who is she? How does she come to power?"

I thought of Margaret Thatcher and wasn't much in the mood to get into details of the political history of the 1970s and '80s. "Never mind. I'll let you find out about her on your own."

"Fair enough."

"And then, there's Queen Elizabeth."

"You mean Princess Elizabeth? Of course, she would become queen at some point. But that's so strange to think about."

"If it seems strange to you, believe me, it's stranger for me to adjust to a world where she's *not* queen. She's been the monarch of Great Britain my entire life and most my mom's as well."

"When does she ascend to the throne, then?"

I paused, not wanting to reveal too much. We were skirting a bit too close to Andrew's own era for my comfort now. "Sooner than you might expect."

"Do you mean—is the King going to die soon?" Andrew frowned, looking a bit upset. "He's still a young man, isn't he?"

"Yes, I suppose he is. Don't worry, he won't die anytime soon. Not in the immediate future. But Elizabeth isn't very old when she becomes queen either."

"Hmm." He thought about this for a moment. I realized I had an opportunity to provide some important advice to Andrew that might help him in the future.

"The King dies of lung cancer, caused by smoking. I probably should have mentioned this earlier, but smoking causes cancer and is very bad for your health. Lots of people die prematurely because of it. Unfortunately, doctors don't discover that for a few more decades."

Andrew looked at me in surprise. "Really? You can die from smoking? Maybe I should cut back my cigarettes a bit."

"Or stop completely? Please?" Andrew didn't smoke that often, but it couldn't hurt to encourage him to get a head start on quitting, could it?

He smiled. "Okay. I've never been a great smoker anyway. I'll try to cut it out. That's a shame about King George, though. He's been a fine leader these past few years, after his brother abdicated."

I nodded. The stress from his role as wartime leader had, undoubtedly, taken its toll on the King's health, too, but I decided not to mention that.

"If it makes you feel better, Elizabeth will be an excellent queen. And one of the longest serving in British history. In 2009, she's still alive and reigning at eighty-three."

He smiled. "That curly-haired little girl is still on the throne in seventy years? Hard to imagine, but good for her."

"Good for all of England, I'd say. And really, she's not that much younger than you. Or I guess she is now. But, you know, when you're ninety-four and she's eighty, it won't seem like much of a difference at all." Of course, that was assuming Andrew survived to reach ninety-four, or anything close to it. I knew the fate of the Queen—a perfect stranger—but not of the most important person in the world to me.

He shook his head in amazement, and lay down again, apparently ready to try to sleep while digesting all the information I'd thrown at him. But I had one last rabbit to pull out of the hat.

"Oh, Andrew? One more thing. Pay attention in the early twenty-first century to a young American politician named Barack Obama."

"And why's that?"

"In 2008, he'll be elected President of the United States." I paused for dramatic effect, savoring the revelation I was about to unveil. "And, by the way—he's black."

I smiled, seeing I'd knocked the wind out of Andrew's sails. He couldn't seem to find anything to say in response to this, so he just shook his head in wonder again.

I was drifting off a few moments later, and I thought Andrew must be asleep, too, as there was complete silence from his side of the bed. But then, so faint that I could barely make them out, I heard him murmur a few words.

"I want to live in your world."

I rolled over, swept the hair back from his forehead and kissed him, murmuring in reply the words I wanted with all my heart to believe, and make him believe as well.

"You will."

18

THE TURN OF EVENTS

I may have excited Andrew's curiosity about the events of the next seven decades, but I certainly hadn't accomplished anything else remotely useful since learning the truth about Molly. I kept thinking, mulling, wracking my brain for a solution to my dilemma, but no matter how much I tried to figure a way out, it wouldn't come.

Should I tell her I thought she should reunite with Patrick? Would it even work if I tried? After all, I didn't even know him (though his blood, as it happened, ran through my veins); I had no real knowledge of their relationship aside from the scraps she'd shared with me. And she didn't exactly seem to be mourning the demise of her engagement. Every time I'd bumped into her in the hospital lately (I was avoiding more prolonged encounters outside work until I figured out what I was going to do, easy enough as work was busy, and I was already spending every free moment with Andrew whenever he was home), she looked quite blithe. A weight seemed to have loosened from her shoulders since telling Patrick she wanted to end things. She appeared to be finally living the life she'd always wanted, as a free and independent woman: the life, it would seem, she was always meant to live.

Except I knew that wasn't true. I knew the future—or rather, I knew the future that was *supposed* to happen. I knew Molly Brennan O'Toole as an old woman in her eighties who had borne six children, buried a husband, and gone to church every Sunday morning of her life. In my mind, I'd always assumed that was the only life she'd ever considered, the only one she could possibly have known.

Maybe all that time, however, she'd been living a lie. Maybe she'd secretly been dreaming of another life, rather than the one she was living as a result of what she'd become: my grandmother. My mother's mother. A woman who'd dedicated her life to taking care of others, not in a hospital but in the confines of her own house.

Every time I thought about all of this, my head hurt. So did my heart. I had, I realized, acted with supreme hubris in telling Molly how she should live her life. But I hadn't acted with any kind of ill intent, just the opposite. I'd seen her as my friend, a young woman at a turning point who needed a nudge from someone with a different perspective to propel her into the life she really wanted to live. In my era, that wouldn't have been seen as selfish at all. I'd been raised by my mother and father to believe I could, and should, be anything I wanted to be when I grew up. Ballet dancer, soap opera actress, teacher, historian—my dreams had changed and evolved over the years, but the whole point was that I was encouraged to dream to begin with. I could choose. I was *expected* to choose.

The idea that I couldn't be anything I wanted to be, within the confines of my own natural abilities, was completely alien to me as a child. And as an adult, I'd carried over that same brazen certainty and applied it to everyone else in my circle, including Molly. She loved nursing. She was excellent at it; she possessed a true gift for healing. And she wasn't ready to settle down and sacrifice her dreams for someone else, even a person that she loved. Why shouldn't she have the same chances I'd always taken for granted, even if she'd happened to have been born sixty-five years earlier?

Yes, it all sounded perfectly logical when I ran these statements through my head. But the problem was, I'd glimpsed a different future. No—I'd lived it. My entire life had been defined and created by the choice Molly made to follow the path she had—or, more accurately, by her lack of freedom to depart from that path. And while the grandmother I had known had appeared far less happy than the cheerful young woman I saw in the hospital hall these days, she'd also given birth to six children, who eventually had twelve children, who had their own dreams, hopes, aspirations. Surely, they all deserved the chance to pursue the lives they wanted, just as much as

Molly did? Surely, they deserved to be alive to pursue them in the first place?

If I let Molly continue on her current path, I'd be dooming myself and all of them, including my own mother—the person I loved most in the world—along with Andrew. When I thought of it that way, I knew I really didn't have a choice. The past—or, for the moment, the future—had to be set right. But how?

The answer came sooner than I expected.

Molly appeared at my flat a week after my conversation with Andrew about the European Union, space travel, and Barack Obama. She pounded on the door (or as close as she would let herself come to pounding, in her inevitably polite fashion) and when I let her in, I could see that she looked frantic.

"Molly, come in. What's wrong?" I asked, shocked at seeing her in such a state.

"Oh, Vivienne," she cried, rushing into my flat and flinging herself on my small sofa, head in her hands. "I don't know what to do. I've made such a mess of things!"

Good to know I'm not the only one, I thought grimly. Apparently, it had not been a banner week or so for the women in our family. "What do you mean? What's wrong?"

"It's Patrick," she gasped, looking up to reveal eyes shining with tears. "He's—he's been hurt."

My heart stopped beating for an uncomfortable few seconds. "Hurt? Hurt how? What happened?"

"There was an accident at his factory. He was running the machine that makes the bullets—I don't know how it works exactly—but somehow there was a small explosion and—"

"Is he all right?" I interjected, unable to restrain myself.

"He—he's got some injuries. But they think he'll be okay if he has someone to take care of him for a few months until he gets back on his feet. But, Vivienne, his whole family is in Ireland! He's got no one here who can do that except—"

I sat down next to her and took her hand in mine. "Except you, you mean?"

She nodded, tears spilling down her face.

"Vivienne, I don't know what to do. I got the message yesterday afternoon after I got home from w-work, and I raced to the hospital to see him. It seems he still had me listed as his person to contact if anything happened on the job. They didn't know we had ended our engagement, so . . ."

"I understand. So, you saw him, and—"

"And it was like all of those feelings from before started coming back. Seeing him that way, bandaged and hurt—" Molly let out a small sob. "I guess, maybe I love him more than I thought I did when I ended things. Or maybe," she reflected, "maybe it's just guilt driving me. The foreman he works under told me he's seemed distracted and glum these past few weeks. I guess that was because I told him I couldn't marry him. So, part of me feels like this is all my fault."

"It's not your fault," I responded fiercely. "Trust me, Molly, it isn't. You're not responsible for what happened to Patrick. It was an accident. They can happen at any time. I mean, my own grandfather—" I stopped myself, but it was too late.

Molly prompted me. "Your grandfather—what about him?"

"He . . . he also had an accident once." I thought quickly, remembering what my mother had told me about it. Her father had been missing part of his finger because of an old injury he'd obtained working on the assembly line during the war, before she was born.

My head was spinning, but at the same time, I felt like everything was becoming clear.

My grandfather—Patrick—had had an injury sustained during his factory work in wartime. Was that the same injury Molly was talking about? If so, that meant he would be okay, which was an enormous relief. But it also meant that his injury had happened in the original timeline he had inhabited before his stupid time-traveling granddaughter showed up in 1939 to ruin his engagement and his life. Did that mean he and Molly were destined to reunite and get married? That their marriage was going to happen regardless, whether I had showed up in Trafalgar Square a year and a half ago or not?

Or was I still somehow unwittingly messing things up? If Patrick had, as his foreman suggested, been distracted at work lately, it hardly seemed too much of a leap to think that his breakup with Molly might be at least a contributing factor. And I had encouraged her to end things, to follow her heart. Maybe his distraction was merely a factor in the accident, but still . . . there it was. It was at least a possibility that my words of advice to Molly had helped lead to this situation, that it wasn't part of his original trajectory. But might this turn of fate also lead to a possible reconciliation that could fix all the damage I'd done over the past few months and set their lives back on their original course, after just a minor detour?

Molly's voice pulled me back to reality. "Vivienne—I just don't know. Should I—should I go back and try to help him through this? Should I—should I marry him after all?"

I took a deep breath to steady myself, aware of how important my next words might be. Molly looked fragile, uncertain—at the pivot point of a major life decision where a friend's advice could tip her over the edge either way.

I wanted to ask her, *What do you want to do?* What is your heart telling you? But I couldn't. I was too afraid of the answer. What if what she really wanted was to walk away from Patrick again, to live the life she'd struggled against the odds to attain and which was now within her grasp? If I knew that for sure, I didn't think I'd have the strength to do what I knew I needed to.

So instead, I said, "It's . . . it's hard for me to say, Molly. And it's not my decision to make, but—it sounds like Patrick needs you now. If you walk away, will you ever feel right about it? Or would you have regrets?"

Regrets. What a word, simple and deceptively small, yet containing multitudes of meaning. I'd spent the last few weeks consumed with more regrets than I'd ever imagined I was capable of feeling. I knew I was about to bring more on myself if Molly took my advice—but I'd feel far more regret if she didn't. Or maybe I'd never be born to feel regret at all. Maybe regret was simply part of the cost of doing business for humans, a transaction fee of sorts for the privilege of being alive.

Molly stared straight ahead, expressionless. I held my breath, waiting for her to speak. As tears spilled down her face, she looked at me again, nodding.

"You're right, Vivienne, of course you're right. I can't abandon him. He needs me. And maybe—maybe I need him as well. Maybe thinking I could live a life on my own, without him, was just foolish. I'm sure it was. I don't know what I was thinking." She shook her head ruefully.

I nodded woodenly, not trusting myself to utter any more words. Molly stood up, looked straight into my eyes, and for the first time since I'd known her—in either lifetime—she put her arms around me and gave me a hug. She broke away quickly, her eyes shiny with tears but managing a slight, wobbly smile.

"Thank you, Vivienne. You've helped me so much. I see now. I see what I need to do."

She moved toward the front door, put her hand on the doorknob, then suddenly turned and looked back at me.

"I have to tell you, Vivienne—you're the best friend I've ever had."

She turned back and walked out the door, shutting it softly but firmly behind her.

I waited until I heard her steps descend the staircase and go out the front door, so I knew she wouldn't be able to hear me. Then I collapsed onto the couch my future grandmother had vacated and let the sobs escape from my body, wrenching me from head to toe, feeling as though they would never stop.

19

TWO WEDDINGS

Marriage is a joyous occasion, they say. Or at least, the ceremony of marriage is supposed to be joyous. I can't say much about the institution itself, never having gotten to experience it properly. But I have to say, my wedding to Andrew was the most joyous day of my life.

But I should back up a bit first. I was not the only member of my family getting married that fall.

Two weeks after Molly visited my flat, she and Patrick were wed. I knew this because I received a lovely invitation in the mail a few days before. Nothing very formal, just a note letting me know when and where the wedding was taking place—at a small Catholic church in central London—and requesting the honor of my presence.

The honor was dubious, as far as I was concerned. In any case, I decided against going, not that it was much of a struggle. Had the circumstances been different, I would have loved to watch my good friend Molly get married to a man she truly loved and wanted to build a life with; nothing would have made me happier than to see her blissful on her wedding day. But as things stood, I knew I couldn't participate. I had done far too much damage to Molly's and Patrick's lives already, I reasoned. I didn't need to take the chance of visiting more trouble on them by showing up at their wedding like some black cloud from a future they couldn't yet see.

Also, I didn't want to see Molly get married. I couldn't, now that I'd been taken into her confidence. I knew too much—about her, about the secret wishes in her heart, which were now about to be buried during a long lifetime of running a household and picking up after six children and a husband until she was widowed at the age of fifty-six. I knew more about Margaret Brennan O'Toole than any person alive ever had; I knew her past, present, and future, and the sacrifices she was making for that future that she would never share with a single living soul. I knew too much to stand there watching her blithely on her wedding day, wishing her the best for a happy, open future. Her future had already been decided—whether by myself, the war, a malfunctioning machine on an assembly line, or forces bigger than all those things combined, I couldn't say. But knowing the end of Molly's story made it too hard for me to watch the beginning, to know it could have gone so many other ways—but now it never would.

So, I did what I felt I had to do. I wrote Molly a note, saying I couldn't attend the wedding due to pressing family business. (I lied, however, and claimed it was Andrew's family.) I sealed up the letter, brought it to the post office, then marched down to the hospital and quit my job. I was determined to remove myself from Molly's life like the contagion I'd turned out to be. I knew she planned to quit the hospital, as well, now that she was getting married, but I didn't want to take any chances of running into her again. Best to exit her life quietly, I reasoned. It was probably cowardly, but that was my decision.

In any case, I doubted the hospital staff would miss me greatly, as I'd been pretty much a disaster as a nurse. The ward sister managed to graciously thank me for my service, while also casting me a slightly disapproving look out of the corner of her eye—look at this young nurse trainee, deserting the war effort when the need for her assistance had never been greater! But I was past the luxury of worrying what other people thought about me and my actions at this point. At least, all other people except for one.

It was a rare sunny-if-cold afternoon in early November when Andrew asked me to be his wife. He was on a break from flying, due to go back up into the skies the following day. We were walking hand in hand through Green Park, and I was surreptitiously casting a glance at Buckingham Palace as we passed, grateful that it was still standing, if somewhat worse for wear since the Blitz had begun. The bombs fell every night, so one had to get outside and make the best of it during the daylight hours. The silence between us was extended but peaceful, until Andrew suddenly broke it.

"You know what, Vivienne?"

"What?" I turned to him, smiling, trying to forget my ruminations on Molly and Patrick and just enjoy this time I had with him while I had it.

"I think we should get married."

The way he put it, it was less a question than a statement of fact, or opinion. *This is what I believe.*

I turned to him, my mouth falling open. "You can't be serious."

"Why not? I love you. You love me. So, we should get married. Seems simple enough." He smiled.

But it was anything but simple, and he knew it. I drew him over to a bench in the park where we could speak quietly, away from any curious onlookers. Not that anyone in London was every terribly curious anyway; it's a city famous for its citizens' determination to keep to themselves. However, I'd noticed that everyone had become a bit more friendly over the past few weeks, talking to strangers during raids and while huddling in bomb shelters, and even sometimes on the street during the day. A new mood of solidarity pervaded the city as we—I was included this time—fought to keep the forces of Nazism at bay and protect our island home.

"Andrew—you know that's not possible. We can't get married."

"And why not?" He tilted his head and smiled at me, daring me to come up with a good reason.

I had plenty. "Well, let's see. I don't have any legal papers that would pass muster for a marriage ceremony, to begin with."

"You must have something. From what you told me—" he glanced around, making sure no one was listening in, "the people who sent you here would have seen to it that you came prepared."

He was right. I did have papers, of a sort—a passport with my name and a fake birthdate on it, which I'd needed to get in and out of Germany back in my child-rescuing days. But I didn't have a birth certificate. Why would I have needed one? I mentioned this glitch to Andrew, who shrugged.

"So, we'll get you one. It's always possible to, you know, buy papers."

I was shocked. "Andrew! You can't be serious. I mean—you're an RAF pilot!"

"That's right, and I'm risking my life for my country every day, gladly. If the worst thing I ever do in my life is to procure some black-market papers so I can marry the woman I love, I think we can call it even."

He had a point, but I was still skeptical. And there was more than paperwork to consider here.

"But Andrew—I don't know. The whole point of marriage is to commit yourself to someone for the rest of your life, and I don't know if I can do that. Not because I don't love you," I added hastily, seeing the expression on his face. "I love you more than anything in the world, you know that! But Andrew, I'm not supposed to be here. I don't know how long I'll be able to stay. Maybe I have an expiration date, maybe I'll just vanish when the war ends—I don't know. I was supposed to leave a year ago. Since I cut myself off from—you know—" I glanced over my shoulder, "I don't know what happens. I don't know if I can just keep living here, surviving in the shadows until someone figures out I don't belong, or if at some point, I'll get yanked back."

"It hasn't happened yet," Andrew argued.

This was true, and I should have been reassured by this, but somehow, I wasn't. Sometimes, when I was out walking the streets, on my way to work or the store or even a bomb shelter, I felt vaguely, creepily, like I was being watched. I wondered if Gunther, or someone else from the Experiment, was still out there somewhere, keeping tabs on me. I couldn't shake the feeling that I wasn't truly free, that I was a piece in a chess game that hadn't played out yet. Looking back, I was surprised I'd been able to walk away so easily.

Andrew tried another line of argument. "Look, maybe what you're saying is true, I don't know. But, Vivienne, look at me! I'm risking my life literally every day. I can't give you a lifetime guarantee either. I don't know what's going to happen to me, any more than you know what's going to happen to you. But I still want to marry you and be with you for as long as I possibly can. I want you to be my wife. I love you, and you love me. And that's all that really matters."

How could I argue with that?

———————————

Our wedding took place two weeks later on a brilliantly sunny autumn day after Andrew returned from his latest assignment in the skies, fighting for England's survival and once more finding the odds in his favor. I didn't know how many more times like this there would be, and I was determined not to dwell on it either. Andrew was right. We were together now, in this moment in time, and that was all we or any of the other couples, families, friends around us could really count on. Best to enjoy it while it lasted, and not overthink things.

It was a small, intimate ceremony. Well, about as intimate as it could possibly be: we eloped. It seemed a practical decision, as we didn't have much time to plan a wedding party and draw up a guest list; we were both keen to make things official as soon as possible, not knowing how long either of us might have to enjoy married life.

I asked Andrew if he minded his family and friends not being there, and he shrugged. His father had died a few years ago, I'd learned; a bad case of pneumonia had carried him off in 1934, the year Andrew finished university. He'd lived long enough to see his son graduate from Oxford, where he himself had gone, and he'd been proud of him. I guess there are worse notes on which to leave this world. His mother lived a quiet life in Sussex, and rarely traveled much these days due to various infirmities. He'd sent her a telegram saying that we were getting married. She sent us back a lovely note and some flowers for the occasion, which was nice, but I never did get a chance to meet her, which made me rather sad. And his brother, his only sibling, was currently stationed in the Pacific on a battleship; a pull to military service clearly ran in the family. So, a nice, quiet elopement it would be.

As for me, I did have family here, and friends, rolled into one unlikely package, but I wasn't going to invite Molly to my wedding any more than I could attend hers. I knew I couldn't deal with the emotions it would bring up. I wanted my wedding day to be one of unvarnished joy, and I wanted it to be about me and Andrew, our happiness in this moment, and whatever the future might hold for us. I knew the end of Molly's story, but I still didn't know the end of mine. In the blessed absence of that knowledge, I just wanted to enjoy my life as much as I could for as long as I was lucky enough to do so.

So, Andrew and I were alone on our wedding day, which was all right with both of us. We began our married life not knowing how long we would have together but, like millions of other people around the world at that moment in history, determined to be together for as long as we could, two people in love in the same time and place.

And so, on a crisp sunny November morning, we officially became husband and wife.

After that, it was only a matter of time. But then, I suppose it always is.

20

THE END

Christmas was coming, but no one felt very jolly. The skies still swarmed with planes, the bombs still fell, and despite the city's almost superhuman heroics in keeping calm and carrying on, it was hard to ignore the fact that London was literally burning night after night.

Nonetheless, Andrew and I spent the first Christmas of our married life together and tried to make it as merry as possible. We managed to procure some duck (goose being out of the question) and some potatoes for the feast on the big day, and I used the last of our ration points to make his favorite dessert, treacle tart. On my birthday two days after Christmas (what would have been the big 3-0 if I were living in my own time, and which Andrew insisted we celebrate despite the rather odd circumstances of my not actually being born for another forty years), he produced a bottle of champagne he had saved from before the war. We were living in his flat now, which was slightly bigger than mine, but still not exactly roomy. Not that we cared. We were together, which was all that mattered, and space was hardly an issue. We both wanted as little space separating us as there could be, for as long as possible.

Two days after my birthday, I received an unexpected visitor. By now, I imagine you can guess who it was.

I opened the door that afternoon to find Molly standing in the hallway, bundled up in a bright blue coat and scarf, rosy-cheeked from the cold. She smiled at me, and I returned the smile, not knowing what exactly to do, but secretly feeling glad to see her as well as surprised.

"Molly, come in!" I ushered her through the door. "How are you? How—how have you been?"

I took a closer look at her. She looked different—somehow older, more mature. She'd always had a serious air to her, but it seemed to have been amplified. Perhaps married life was already having an impact on her, just a few months in. She was still plainly a young girl, pretty and fresh-faced, but I thought I could detect traces in her face of the older woman she was to become, the one I would eventually know. Though truth be told, I knew the younger version of Molly far better than I would ever know the elderly one. And despite all the years that stretched ahead, I knew there was nothing I could do to change that now, and it made me sad. By the time I returned to the world of 2009—if I ever did—Molly would already be gone.

"I'm fairly well," she replied, removing her scarf and turning to look at me. She met my gaze steadily, and her expression was unreadable. Was she unhappy? Resigned? At peace with her decisions? I honestly couldn't tell.

"How are you? Congratulations to you and Andrew."

"Thank you," I said with a smile, which I wiped away immediately. Smiling somehow felt inappropriate in the circumstances.

"I was so pleased to get your note. I'm sorry I couldn't be there for the wedding."

"Well, as I said, we decided to elope. Andrew's family wasn't able to make it, and, well, it just seemed simpler, with the war on and all."

"I understand completely," she said, twirling her hat in her hands and looking a little uncomfortable.

"Is anything wrong?" I asked her tentatively.

"No, nothing's wrong. Actually, I have some news I wanted to share with you . . . that's why I've come. I'm going to have a baby."

Of course, she was. It was December 1940, and my mother was born in August 1941—Molly's first child. I could do the math, but it still was an odd feeling to hear her speak these words and to know that, for the first time since I'd been back in the London of the Second World War, my mother had entered the picture. She was in the room, literally (a bizarre thought, if ever there was one), but her presence filled it metaphorically as well. My mom—the reason I'd done what I'd done and pushed

Molly ever so slightly into making a decision she might not have made on her own. Or maybe she would have. I'll never know.

"That's wonderful news," I said, managing a smile for her. It *was* wonderful news, of course. Not just for me, but for my dad, and for the countless people my mom would touch in the course of her life as a nurse, a mother, a wife, and a friend. My mother was coming into existence; it was official. It made the bleakness of the world we were living in at the moment feel more tolerable, the sacrifices that had been made easier to justify. My mother's life, I told myself, would be worth every price anyone had ever paid.

Molly smiled and nodded her thanks. Clearly, she had not come here for emotional displays. She just wanted to share the news with me, as a friend. She couldn't begin to grasp the impact it would have on me, and I thought it would be unwise to tip her off.

"Would you like anything? A cup of tea, maybe?"

"No, thanks. I can't stay. Patrick's waiting for me."

"Let me walk you out then."

"All right. Thank you, Vivienne."

We headed outside together, both lost in our separate thoughts.

―――――――――

It was a gloomy winter's day. I walked silently alongside Molly as we headed to the Underground, shivering a bit from the cold, damp air. Something was nagging at me, some stray thought in the back of my mind that I couldn't pull up from the depths of memory. It was Molly who reminded me of what I'd forgotten.

"Oh, Vivienne, I meant to wish you a happy birthday. I'm sorry I didn't say so earlier; I know it was just a few days ago. Today's the twenty-ninth, isn't it?"

I nodded. "That's right, it is. Thank you." It was thoughtful of her to remember, especially with everything else she had going on in her life. And, I reflected, my thank you really carried more weight than I had intended. After all, if not for her, there wouldn't have been a birthday for me to celebrate at all. But obviously, she could never know that. There were so many things about me and my life that she could never know.

I suddenly stopped short as the stray thought from before struck me with full force. Today was December 29, 1940. My memory for historical dates had never failed me yet during my time in London, and I couldn't believe I was only now remembering the significance of this one.

A passage from my dissertation, burned into my brain through endless hours of writing and rewriting, suddenly burst back into my head.

"December 29, 1940, saw one of the worst firebombings of London during the Blitz. Beginning at 6:30 p.m., 100,000 bombs were dropped on London, killing 160 people, injuring 250 others, and causing significant damage to the city, including a direct hit to St. Paul's Cathedral, which was fortunately saved from destruction through the efforts of the St. Paul's Watch. Due to the massive destruction in its wake, the bombing was called 'The Second Great Fire of London.'"

Quickly, I glanced at my watch. It was 6 p.m. I'd lost track of time, and night had fallen without my really noticing.

"Molly," I blurted out, suddenly feeling panic begin to rise within my chest, "Why did you decide to come here today?

She looked at me in surprise. "Well, just to see you. And congratulate you on your marriage and tell you about the baby."

"There was no other reason?" She looked at me, baffled, and shook her head.

"I mean, no other reason at all? You don't have an errand to run nearby? You aren't stopping off to see anyone else? The only reason you came out today was to visit me?"

She nodded, looking completely confused.

I didn't have time to think. All I knew was I had to get my grandmother—and mother—out of here and to safety as soon as possible.

"Molly, I need you to do something for me, right now. Please, go home, back to Patrick, and stay inside all evening. Promise me you won't go out for anything." I knew where she and Patrick lived, and it was nowhere near the part of the city where the bombs were about to fall. But if she had come out today, to another part of town, solely to see me, and to give me her news . . . if there was nothing else that had impacted her choice. . . .

My grandmother had survived the Second Great Fire of

London once. But now I was terrified that, because she'd made the choice to visit me, she might not be so lucky this time.

Molly looked at me as if I'd lost my mind, but I didn't care. "Please, Molly, just go. Do this for me. Go home and stay there. I have—I have a bad feeling about this. It's getting dark, the German bombers could show up soon—something just feels off tonight, you know what I mean? Call it a premonition, but I just need you to get home and to know you're safe."

She still looked puzzled but nodded. "All right, Vivienne, I will. But what about you? You shouldn't stay out either. Go on and get back to your flat. Where's Andrew tonight?"

"Flying." I couldn't even think about that right now, about the possibilities that awaited him up in the sky. "Please, Molly, go now. Please!"

She nodded solemnly and leaned over and kissed my cheek. "All right. I'll go right home. Feeling a bit tired anyway, in my condition . . ." Her voice trailed off. "But I'll see you soon, won't I?"

"Of course," I promised recklessly. "I'll see you soon. I promise."

She nodded, smiled at me one last time, and crossed the street toward the Underground station. In another minute, she was gone, protected under the earth until she could get home to safety, away from the calamity that was about to rain down from the skies.

I should have left then, too. I was going to. But I

couldn't help stopping for one last glimpse of London before the destruction began, before the Second Great Fire began to burn.

I leaned back against a building, my gaze swiveling to take in the scene around me. My wanderings had taken me farther than I intended, and I was now somewhere in Holborn. St. Paul's Cathedral was visible in the distance. Everything was still calm, deceptively peaceful. No sign yet of the fiery holocaust I knew was coming.

I thought I only stood there for a minute, taking in the scene, trying to freeze London forever as it was in my mind at this moment. But time got away from me, as it has a habit of doing.

Suddenly, I heard a noise—loud, whirring, buzzing. I'd heard it before, of course, but I'd always been lucky before, like most of the people of London. The bombs had always missed me.

But now, staring up at the sky and the source of the noise—a handful of Luftwaffe planes soaring overhead, announcing the start of the evening's bloodshed—I realized that my luck might be about to run out.

I ran as fast as I could toward the nearest Underground station to take refuge, to join all the other people who hadn't known this was coming. I'd had the advantage over all of them, but it hadn't helped me in the end—6:30 p.m. had arrived sooner than I had thought possible.

I could see the station across the street, promising safety or at least its illusion, but I heard the loud whirring above my head and suddenly felt the stabbing certainty that I was not going to make it in time.

Then I heard an explosion, felt myself lifted off my feet, and slammed into something hard.

Andrew, I thought fleetingly. *Will he know where I am? Will he know how to find me? Will I ever see him again?*

Those were my last coherent thoughts in London of 1940.

Interlude

I opened my eyes. My head should have hurt—I expected it to—but it didn't. I looked around.

I was lying in what looked like a white hospital bed, though it was more comfortable than I might have expected. As my eyes adjusted to the bright white light, I saw that the room, or space, was barren. In fact, there didn't seem to be anything solid in my line of vision; just the bed I was lying in and a shroud of light mist for a background.

I thought at first I must be in a hospital somewhere, and my mind jumped forward to Andrew. Did he know where I was? Who had found me? How had I survived?

But the more I took it all in, the room didn't look like any part of the hospitals I'd spent so much time in over the past few months. And I didn't feel like I'd just survived a fiery inferno of a bombing. I felt surprisingly okay.

I thought I was alone and might have preferred it remain that way while I sorted all of this out. But the next thing I knew, a familiar voice spoke behind me.

"So, Vivienne, we meet again."

I recognized owner of the voice and turned my head, staring at him in surprise.

Gunther stood next to my bedside, regarding me with a look that was hard to define. But I wasn't terribly interested in trying, or in figuring out how he'd gotten here. I had a few questions I wanted answered right away.

"What's going on? Where am I?"

"That's not important," replied Gunther, his eyes boring coolly into mine. Still the master of minimal detail, apparently, and still seeing fit to determine what I should and shouldn't know.

But I wasn't in the mood to argue with him. I had too many things I needed his help to sort out.

"Well then—how did I get here? What happened after the bombing started, and I hit my head? I think I must have passed out, and—"

With a trace of impatience, Gunther cut across me. "Yes, you did. However, you suffered no permanent injury. I trust you feel well?"

I nodded, puzzled. "Yes, I do. I feel fine. But how is that possible? After the bombing . . ."

My voice trailed off, and I looked at Gunther expectantly. His familiar expression of mild contempt crossed with disbelief at my simplicity was back in place. But before he could answer me, other questions came flooding into my brain in rapid succession.

"Andrew—and Molly? Where are they? Are they okay?"

"Well, Vivienne, that is a complicated question. The question of how and where they are is, after all, largely contingent on *when* they are."

"I don't know what you mean."

"Certainly, you do. If you want me to answer your question, you need to phrase it correctly."

I paused for a moment; I thought I felt a headache beginning after all as I struggled under the weight of what I was trying to fathom. Then I understood what he was asking me to ask him.

"How are Molly and Andrew on December 30, 1940?"

I held my breath, waiting for his response.

"Molly O'Toole made it back to her home before the bombing started, thanks in part to your warning. She and her husband survived the bombing of London that night, and all the subsequent ones over the next four and a half years. On August 28, 1941, she gave birth to her first child, a girl she named Elizabeth."

My mother. I nodded, exhaling as if the weight of the world had fallen off my shoulders. Molly was okay. So was my mother. I hadn't screwed their futures up after all.

"And . . . and Andrew?"

"He also survived the bombing and was alive on December 30, 1940."

"And after that?"

"You certainly want to know everything, don't you? Very well. He survived the war, retired from the RAF once it was over, and became a history professor at Oxford for several decades."

I felt tears prick my eyes, thinking of Andrew. He had made it; he had survived the war. My glory boy had lived to see the peace he had risked so much to give to the world.

"But—what happened to me? I mean, I'm here— wherever here is—and not back there with them. Does that mean I died?"

For the first time since our conversation began, Gunther's contemptuous attitude faded, and he looked at me soberly. He appeared to be thinking deeply, as if trying to find the right words to answer my question.

"Death, Vivienne, is a tricky concept. By that I mean, death represents the end of a person's natural life. A person born in 1915, for example, like Molly, might expect to live eighty, eighty-five years if she is lucky. Then her body will wear out, it will die, and she will exist no more—at least, on this planet. What happens after that, I can't begin to tell you. It is a subject for philosophers and religion, not scientists and time travelers."

I started to speak, and he held up his hand to stop me.

"Your situation, as I'm sure you can grasp, is different from Molly's, or Andrew's, or that of anyone else who was born at the time they were. You were born in 1980. You technically did not exist at all in 1940 and would not be born yet for another forty years. You were only ever in that time under very special circumstances; it was not your own. As I tried to tell you many times," he added, a bit of his old contemptuousness finding its way back into his voice.

"And so, to answer your question—you did not die in 1940. You could not, because you were never really there. Your corporeal body could suffer no real harm as long as the seeds of your future self remained safely in place, waiting for their time to bloom."

He smiled wryly. And I thought I understood what he was saying. When Molly and I parted on my final day in London and she headed home, she had carried to safety not just herself, but my own mother, tucked away inside her. In taking shelter, she had kept both of them safe. And my mother, in turn, was able to be born and eventually bring me into the world decades later. As long as Molly lived, I was tethered to life. She had kept me safe in the future, even if she couldn't protect me from the impact of a falling building on that day.

"I understand," I said, nodding. I thought about Molly, and how much I owed her. And how I would never be able to see her again and thank her for all she had given me, at such great cost.

"And so . . . now what?"

For the second time, Gunther spoke the words I had once dreaded hearing. "It's time for you to go home."

But this time, I didn't feel the same sense of dread. Sadness, yes, at what and whom I was leaving behind. But I knew he was right. I had done all I could. I had used up my time in this world which, as he correctly pointed out, had never been my own. It was time to return to the one that was.

I nodded. "Okay. I'm ready."

He didn't comment, just held out his hand. The small, bright object he'd shown me before was visible again. "Where exactly are we going?"

"Back to the beginning."

But a circle has no beginning, I thought as I clasped my hand around the miniature Delorean. I wasn't going back to the beginning; that was long before I'd been born, before even Molly had been born. I was simply going back to my starting place; to somewhere in the middle. It was time to try to pick up the pieces and figure out my next steps.

It was time, finally, for me to go home.

PART THREE

21

THE REUNION

April 28, 2009

The nurse looked up in surprise when she saw the young woman at the visitor's desk. She had been informed by the day's guest log that a family member would be coming to see the patient in Room 308, but she had been expecting someone . . . older. However, she greeted the girl warmly and walked her down the hall to the room.

"I'm glad he's got a visitor," she commented to the young woman, who was not much older than the nurse herself. She wondered what had brought her to see the old man, what connection there might be between them. She had long had the impression that he had no children, grandchildren, or family of any sort, since he rarely received visitors, and it made her sad. He was such a nice gentleman, unfailingly polite and courteous, and she was pleased that he would have some company for a change.

The young woman nodded, not commenting on the nurse's words or elaborating on the reasons for her presence at the Sunny Acres nursing home that day. A few minutes later, they had reached the room and the nurse opened the door and entered.

"Mr. Sheffield? You have a visitor. A young lady named…"

She had forgotten the guest's name and turned toward her to ask, but before she could, the girl stepped into the room, staring straight into the old man's face. And she heard him respond, in his low, somewhat raspy voice, "I know who she is."

The girl walked into the room, towards the patient, and the nurse could see she was no longer needed. "Very well. I'm down the hall at the desk. Just buzz me if you need anything." With a quick smile, she backed out of the room and shut the door quietly behind her.

The girl walked slowly toward the elderly man, never taking her eyes off his. He stared at her face almost hungrily, as if it were one he had been waiting a lifetime to lay his eyes on again.

He reached out his hand, and she stepped nearer. He ran his fingers down the side of her face, his eyes staring directly into hers, as memories flooded into his still-sharp mind that, for better or worse, remembered everything.

Finally, he broke the silence, and spoke the words he had waited nearly seventy years to utter.

"I knew you'd come."

22

THE LETTER

For the next few months, Andrew and I were inseparable.

Of course, the experience was different for each of us. In Andrew's case, he had waited a lifetime—nearly seventy long years—to see me again. For me, the timeline had been collapsed, and I felt as if I had seen him only days ago—which indeed I had. Andrew had not died on that day in December 1940, thank God. He had survived the Second Great Fire of London, and the rest of the war, and gone on to live a rather extraordinary life afterward. A life without me.

I had so much I wanted to ask him. I'd only lived a few weeks since the last time we'd seen one another, when I'd casually said goodbye to him that morning before he left to hop in his plane to try and save the world. But he had survived the battle, and he was still here to tell the tale. Many, many tales, in fact.

I listened in fascination as my husband poured out his stories of the past seventy years, a full lifetime I knew nothing about except what I'd managed to glean from his sparse hospital record when I'd tracked him down.

It would take far too long to tell all of Andrew's story, and I could never do it justice anyway. So, I'll just stick to the main facts.

He served in the RAF for the rest of the war. In 1944, he was transferred from London to Southeast Asia, where he flew in the China-Burma-India theater for the last year of the conflict. He had a few narrow escapes—his plane was nearly shot down once by a Japanese pilot—but apparently it had been his lucky day and not his enemy's, for he managed to emerge unscathed ("the landing was a bit rough, though . . . did end up with a few cuts and bruises, but nothing to speak of, really").

When the war was over, he gave serious thought to what to do next. He was only thirty-three in 1945, still relatively young, and he could have kept on flying for a few more years. But he knew it would never be the same as those exhilarating moments soaring in the skies over Britain, fighting for the homeland whose green fields he could see below. He didn't want to spend the rest of his life as an aging glory boy, looking back on his magical youth and telling stories about days gone by that could never be recovered. He realized his flying days were done, and it was time to move on.

And yet, what he chose to do next did involve telling stories, just of a different sort. He returned to the university where he'd taught before the war and took up his old post as a history professor for a few years. His focus had been the nineteenth century—for him, the recent past. But now more of the world's story had unfolded, the twentieth century filling in and taking on more color and shade, and he wanted to connect the dots for his students, encourage them to see how the past he'd once studied in school had led to the global conflict that had inspired him to take to the skies.

Moreover, he wanted to help shape a better world for the next generation. He didn't want any of the young men (and later, women) he taught to have to make the same choice he once had: to give up or postpone their dreams because they needed to serve their country and save it from potential destruction. He wanted to live far enough into the future to see the world I'd once sketched for him as we lay in bed that one sleepless night, to live long enough to teach young men and women who'd never have to worry about the threat of a European war that had hung over both his father's generation and his own.

He was an excellent teacher and soon realized this work was what fulfilled him at this stage of life, just as being a pilot had during his twenties. In the early 1950s, he was recruited once again by the same old professor who'd encouraged him to join the RAF in his youth. But this time, he accepted a position as a full professor at Oxford, where he taught until his retirement forty years later.

As for the rest of his life, he'd dated a bit but had never come close to marriage again. When people asked him in later years about his past, he simply said he was a widower and left it at that, not feeling the need to provide any further details.

"You never met anyone else, in all that time?" I asked him hesitantly. I wasn't sure what answer I wanted to hear. A selfish part of me wanted him to reply that, of course, he'd never met anyone in seven decades who could compare to me. But another part of me was saddened at the thought of him spending all those years alone.

"I didn't need to," he replied, squeezing my hand. "I'd already found my wife. And I knew something no one else could know—that someday, even if it was far in the future, you'd be coming back to me."

For in all the time we'd been apart, as he told me in the first flush of our reunion on that April afternoon, he had never given up hope that he would see me again.

"I knew I just had to keep waiting," he explained to me, clasping my hands in his and staring at me with his familiar earnest expression that I knew so well. "I knew that if I could hold on long enough, you'd come and find me."

And he was right; I had. Any other business I had to resume in the twenty-first century could wait. Finding Andrew, seeing the love of my life again, and spending all the time with him that I possibly could, was all that was on my mind now.

Because once again, I knew we were facing a ticking clock.

The difference was that this go-round, the person whose time was running short in this world was not me.

I'll get back to that in a moment. But first, I want to mention something Andrew showed me after I returned to his nursing home the next day, as I would for every day of the next several months. Actually, two things.

"I saved these for you," he announced immediately when I showed up promptly at 8 a.m. on that second morning. The sun was streaming into his window; London's weather was, for once, acting in a proper spring-like manner. It was almost as if the weather itself could sense what was happening, the joyful scenes that were taking place within these walls.

"I'm sorry, I completely forgot about them yesterday," he added apologetically, as if a ninety-seven-year-old man was to blame for not having a perfect memory. "In all the excitement of seeing you again, you know . . ."

He handed me an envelope, containing what I realized was a news clipping. I unfolded it, and when I read it, my eyes teared up a bit (I hoped I would not repeat the bout of joyful crying I'd experienced yesterday).

It was the front page of the *Guardian* from November 5, 2008, the day after Barack Obama had been elected president of the United States. The headline at the top read, "Barack Obama to Be America's First Black President: George Bush and John McCain Praise

Democratic Winner as Record Numbers Turn Out to Vote in Historic Election."

"I saved it for you," he said, smiling. "A little piece of history . . . and you gave me quite a bit of advance notice! For nearly seventy years I waited for this, but it was still amazing when the day finally came. For the last four years, I've been telling everyone I met that this young Obama fellow would be president one day. Hardly any of them believed me at first, but I got the last word there!"

He chuckled, reaching for the clipping and putting it carefully back into his drawer. I laughed, too, smiling through my tears, so happy he had lived to see this moment in history. I was glad I'd told him, even if it had spoiled the surprise.

"And here's something else—something a bit more personal. I received this four years ago. I figured you'd want to see it too."

I looked down at the letter. It was addressed to Andrew in an unfamiliar hand. I opened it up and began reading. And this time, there was no possible way to stop myself from crying.

"Dear Mr. Sheffield,

Please allow me to introduce myself. My name is Lillian Spencer Wallace, and I live in Devon. I obtained your address through the Oxford University alumni network (my husband is also an Oxford graduate) and hope that you will not mind me reaching out and contacting you to share my story.

Two years ago, my mother passed away. I had known from her and my father that I had been adopted as a very small child, though I had no memory of it. However, they shared only a minimal amount of detail with me about my history. When my mother died, it fell to me to go through her papers and clean house, and that was when I stumbled upon some documents that explained my story in much greater detail.

Until that time, I had no idea that I was born in Germany, to Jewish parents. I had even less of an inkling that these same parents had made the choice to have me smuggled out of pre-war Germany in 1939 to be sent to live with, and eventually be adopted by, a British family. As a mother myself, I cannot even begin to imagine how difficult this decision must have been for them. But I realize I almost certainly owe my life to their selfless choice to send me out of Nazi Germany to freedom in England.

As I dug deeper into my background, I discovered that I was not alone. During that dark period of history, a number of other Jewish families in Germany sent their children to England before war broke out. There was a secret network set up to smuggle these children out of the country, which was composed both of brave Germans and equally brave men and women of other countries who came to Germany to rescue them and bring them to safety.

Through various notes and papers, I was able to discover the name of the young woman who rescued me—Vivienne Riley. And after digging a bit further, I discovered that she married Andrew Sheffield in 1940, and, tragically, died a few months later during the Blitz in London.

I cannot even begin to fathom the bravery of this young woman—your wife. I cannot imagine what may have compelled her to travel into Nazi Germany on the eve of war to save children she had never met, had no connection with, and would never see again. But I know that it is only due to her bravery and compassion that I am alive today.

I have lived a wonderful life. I had a lovely childhood with my adoptive parents and have been married to a young man I met in my hometown for nearly fifty years. We have four children and seven grandchildren. I could not be happier with how my life has turned out, and I cannot express to you my gratitude for those who risked so much to ensure I would be able to live such a happy one.

I wish to offer you my deepest sympathies for your wife's death. It must have been a terrible blow to lose her so young, and so soon after your marriage. I am sure you still miss her, even after so many years have passed.

So, if you will forgive my rambling—I wanted to write to you to express my thanks, very belatedly, to Vivienne, and to assure you that her life, though cut tragically short, was not lived in vain. She was a savior to myself and, I am sure, many other children like me who might otherwise have met horrible fates. And I am sure that in *even the limited time the two of you shared, she brought you tremendous joy. May she never be forgotten.*

Sincerely and wishing you all the best,
Lillian Spencer Wallace"

I looked up at Andrew, my face covered in tears, not trusting myself to speak. Lillian. That beautiful little girl I had met in Germany all those years ago! I could still see her blond curls, her chubby, rosy cheeks. I could remember the feel of her tiny hand grasping my own as I pulled her to safety as best as I could. And now she was a grandmother, in her seventies, with a full life behind her. I was so happy to know how things had turned out for her, to learn the rest of her story, and yet somehow, I felt consumed with a sadness I couldn't quite name.

I had been dropped into Lillian's life by the Experiment. They had given me the opportunity to save her, and I had done so. Did that one act, and the lives of the other children I had rescued, make my return to the past worthwhile? Did it justify everything else that had happened—falling in love with Andrew and then abandoning him for nearly the entirety of his life? Befriending Molly, showing her a way to realize a dream and find happiness, just to quash it to keep myself and others I loved alive in a future she couldn't yet see?

I didn't know the answers to these questions. I looked back on the year and a half I had spent in that dark, nightmarish period of history that was not my own. I tried to assess it as soberly and detachedly as someone Andrew's age might, looking back on his long, full life. I had done some good. I had done some harm. I could only hope, in the end, that the former had outweighed the latter.

I glanced down at the letter, then up into Andrew's eyes—faded somewhat now, lined with wrinkles, the eyebrows turned white long ago—but still the same eyes I remembered. He smiled at me, and I read the message in them that he was sending me: I had done my best. That was enough. It had to be.

23

ASHES TO ASHES

Andrew died the following autumn—October 12, 2009.

There's not much more to say about that, and I really don't want to talk about it. When old people die, we comfort ourselves—or try to—with the knowledge that they lived long, full lives and hopefully passed into the next world peacefully, with no regrets. I knew Andrew better than anyone, in so many ways, and I can honestly say that was the case for him. He lived an extraordinary life. He regretted nothing he had done, nor anything he hadn't done. I know this because he told me.

And yet his death left a hole in my heart like nothing else ever had. It's still too painful to discuss, really. In any case, grief is a boring topic. Everyone goes through it, or if they haven't yet, they will. It's always waiting around the corner. I can't add anything new to that conversation that hasn't already been said many times over.

Andrew, of course, knew it was coming. He'd cheated death many times, flying his Spitfire all those years ago to protect his country and save the world from the Nazis. He'd long since made his peace with the idea that his time on earth could well be short, as it was for so many of his friends. He was lucky; he made it out alive and went on to new adventures and experiences. He survived until ninety-seven—an extraordinary achievement in itself—all the while waiting for me to show up.

"You don't know how hard it was for me, once I knew you were alive," he told me one afternoon as we sat out on the back porch of the nursing home, holding hands and enjoying the afternoon sunshine together. "I knew I could find you if I looked hard enough—what with the internets and everything that they have now that you told me about all those years ago." (I smiled.) "But I couldn't bring myself to search for you. I knew I'd probably just terrify you if I showed up on your doorstep one day—an unfamiliar, ancient, withered fellow like me, prattling on about time travel and the fact that we were once married during the war? No, that would never do. I knew I had to wait for you to come to me."

"And you knew I would." I sighed, resting my head on his shoulder. "I'm so glad I wasn't too late."

He turned to me and smiled. "Not to worry, Vivienne. I didn't wait seventy years to see you again to drop dead before you reappeared. I held on, for you, no matter what life threw at me."

His expression sobered, and he took my hand. "Now, Vivienne, there's something we need to talk about."

I knew where he was going with this and wanted no part of it. I looked down and shook my head.

"After I'm gone . . ."

"No . . ."

"Yes. We have to talk about this. I know I don't have much longer; I can feel the end coming closer every day. And I'm at peace with it. I'll miss you, of course—but then, I've had lots of practice at that." He smiled, despite the sadness in his eyes.

I couldn't think of anything to say, so I said nothing.

"And I don't want to talk about me now. It's you I'm thinking of. Because after I'm gone, I want you to go on."

"Of course, I will," I replied dully. "I won't have much choice, will I?"

"I mean really go on, Vivienne. Not just endure, but live. Thrive. I want you to be happy. I want you to live a long life, to continue to be in this world long after I'm gone from it, and to fully embrace all the magic that comes with that. I had my time, and I did my best with it. This is your time. You're a young woman, and you deserve a full life. And if you should meet someone . . ."

"No." I shook my head vehemently. That was out of the question, and I couldn't believe he would even raise it, now, during what we both knew were likely our last days together.

"Vivienne, I want you to be happy."

"I am! I was!"

"Yes, we were happy together. But soon I'll be gone, and I want you to have more than memories to bring you happiness. I want you to be happy here and now. It may take a while, but I know you can do it. You must do it."

His tone was firm, as if he would brook no arguments from me on this subject.

"But Andrew—I couldn't. I can't even think of being with anyone else—after you . . ." I broke off, choking back the tears that were threatening to erupt. "I mean—you waited for me! All those years—you never got married or had children with anyone else. You could have moved on from me—I wouldn't have blamed you if you had—but you didn't. So, how can I consider moving on from you?"

"But there's a difference, Vivienne. I knew you were coming, eventually, and that if I held on long enough, I'd see you again. And in all those years, I had that thought to keep me going. I never met another woman I fancied marrying and having a family with, anyway, so I never felt like it was a loss. But it's different for you. My end is drawing near, and I won't be reappearing in seventy years' time. When I'm gone, that will be it—for a while at least. Until we meet in the next world. But in this one, I want you to live and be happy. I need you to; otherwise, how will I ever be able to rest?"

I shook my head, feeling my tears spill as it moved from side to side. Childishly, I protested, "You never used to talk to me like this when we were the same age."

He laughed, then said soberly, "No, I didn't. But since I last saw you, I've lived many years and learned many things about life and about myself. I know more about the world, about life and death and grief and loss, than you do, Vivienne. You'll learn it all one day—everyone does. But until then, you're a young woman with her whole life still ahead of her, and that's how I want you to act. As if you believe, every day, that the best is yet to come."

I didn't believe it. I couldn't. But when Andrew spoke to me in a certain way—laying out what he knew to be right, and making it seem like the only option—I had never been able to argue with him. That was why I had agreed to marry him all those years ago, and while that had been a ridiculous idea in many ways, I still couldn't think of it as anything other than the best decision of my life. I knew he was right again now, even if I couldn't yet wrap my head around what he was saying. But as he pointed out, he'd had a seventy-year head start on all of this. Someday, perhaps, I would catch up with him in maturity and wisdom. He just wouldn't be here to see it.

I turned to him, my eyes brimming again, but managed to hold back the tears this time as I fixed him with my most determined look. "OK, Andrew. I promise."

———

When he died a few months later, holding my hand, that was Andrew's final word: "Promise."

And my last words to him were the same ones I'd spoken in that church in London in November 1940, while the world was blowing up around us and the future seemed utterly uncertain to anyone who didn't know how it was going to end: "I do."

24

A CIRCLE HAS
NO BEGINNING

The weeks after Andrew's death were a haze. I don't really have many memories of them, which is probably for the best. But by the time he'd been in the ground for a month, I had managed to do two things—both small, but to me, they felt important.

The first was to sign up for an online dating site. I hated the very thought of it. I wanted no man but the one I had just laid to rest. But I had promised him I would try to move forward, to find happiness, possibly, with someone new. I felt obliged to follow through on my word.

I still haven't uploaded a photo or written one of those stupid paragraph-long bios or filled out a composite of my likes and dislikes for the algorithm to deal with. But at least I signed up. One baby step at a time.

The other thing I did was to call my mother and ask her a question I'd been wondering about for quite a while.

As our phone call was wrapping up (and I tried to hide the depth of my sadness, since I couldn't begin to explain any of it to her, which made me feel awful), I asked her, "Mom? I was wondering . . . how did you choose my name?"

She paused, apparently surprised by the question, and after a moment replied, "You know, now that I think back on it—it was your grandmother's idea."

"My grandmother?" My heart rate quickened. "What do you mean?"

"My mother, your Grandmother O'Toole. Well, you know, she and I didn't always have the easiest relationship." I heard my mother sigh slightly on the other end of the line. "We still made a point of talking every few weeks though, even after I moved to America. Mostly it was rather tedious, if not downright unpleasant at times—nothing I was doing with my life seemed to please her. But I remember when I called to tell her I was pregnant with you. I could tell she was really pleased, even though she wasn't given to big emotional displays—well, I'm sure you remember that about her."

"Yes," I whispered. "And—and what about my name?"

"Well, as I said, I told her I was pregnant, and we had a nice conversation about it. It made a lovely change, really. And I asked her—just making conversation, or maybe I was trying to make her feel included in what was happening in my life—if she had any ideas for a name. I was planning to just file away whatever she said, maybe use it as a middle name if I didn't absolutely hate it, but she surprised me. She said, 'How about Vivienne?'

"I thought it was a beautiful name, and I told her so. And I asked what made her think of it. She told me—" My mother sighed again, this time sounding a bit sorrowful.

"Told you what?"

"Well, I guess Vivienne was the name of a friend she'd had, many years ago. Back during the war, before I was born. And she died—I'm not sure how exactly—if she was killed in the war or died of something else. I didn't want to ask. But I thought that was so sad, this poor girl dying and my mother losing a friend so young. She never had many friends that I can remember; I think it was hard for her to open up to people."

"Yes," I whispered as the pieces began to click into place.

"Anyway, I thought it was a lovely name, and I told her I'd use it. And a few months later, you were born. I remember I sent her a photo of you when you were a newborn, and she wrote back, 'Vivienne is beautiful.'"

I could feel my mother smiling over the phone. "Which you were, of course. It was one of the few times in my relationship with my mother where we were on the same page together, where I actually felt like I'd done something right in her eyes. I was so glad I'd chosen that name for you. She was right; it was absolutely perfect."

I hung up the phone a few moments later, my head still spinning and tears beginning to prick in my eyes again. It felt strange to feel sadness over anything other than Andrew's death, but here I was.

Well, damn.

25

GOING HOME

The next few months saw quite a few changes in my life.

In May 2010, after returning to America following Andrew's death, my dissertation was finally approved, and I received my doctorate. I had put my studies on hold to spend as much time with Andrew as I could while he was alive, sending constant assurances to my university advisor back home that I was simply doing some extra, last-minute research in London to add to the body of work I'd amassed over the past few years and would return with an improved product once I'd finished. In reality, I no longer cared about my dissertation, but I'd come this far, and I've always believed in following through on things. It was a lesson in tenacity that my mother had instilled in me since I was a child, and it's true—old habits do die hard. And in the days and nights after Andrew passed away, which felt so endless as I attempted to figure out how to begin to navigate life without him, my studies had been something of a salve, a much-needed distraction, even if the subject matter was a bit too close to my heart now to make it function as a fully immersive escape. However, I ploughed on, finished my writing, and submitted my completed paper just in time to make the cutoff for Spring 2010 graduation from my doctoral program.

And so, on a sunny, warm day in May 2010, I officially became Dr. Vivienne Riley. After having spent my entire (linear) adult life waiting for that moment, I must say that when it came, it felt quite anticlimactic. Partly, this was because I was living through the aftermath of so many things, so weighted down by grief that happiness, even as a result of a hard-won achievement, was hard to come by. But there was more to it than that.

When your life changes, your world changes, and so does your perspective. You perceive and filter the happenings of your life through a different lens than you did before. In my case, from the day I discovered my first Little House on the Prairie book at age six up until April 2009, I'd been obsessed with history—its broad sweep, its minute details, how the past could shape and impact the present. But until I accepted my assignment on that spring day when I met Gunther, I didn't really understand what all of that could actually mean, not in theory but in practice.

I was given a degree for studying, writing about, and interpreting history. I'd done that well. It had always been my strength, my greatest talent. But now, my perspective had shifted with my experiences. I had traveled back into what I'd once known as "history" and helped shape it, for better or worse. This fact didn't make me feel proud; rather, I felt unsettled, as if the ground had shifted beneath my feet when I wasn't looking. Because if I could make this kind of difference, for good or for ill, what actions were other people taking in that same past to change the course of history as we know it as of June 2010?

Because of my decision on a spring day in 2009, Andrew, Molly, Lillian, and possibly many other people had had their own lives altered permanently in a past before I was born. Realizing this, I couldn't see history as a solid, academic subject anymore, even a very compelling one that had always brimmed with life. It now felt moving, ever-changing, and uncertain. I felt that I had built my professional life on a castle made of sand, which at any moment could be swept away by a powerful wave.

And even though I had returned to my own natural timeline to resume my own life, I couldn't stop thinking about how the Experiment continued—more people being recruited to go back and change a past that was still fluid and malleable, if you could find your way back to it. Would they ever succeed in their ultimate goal and wipe the Second World War from the history books? I still couldn't imagine this was possible, since the history books I read looked the same as they had before—minus a few people I personally knew, whose trajectories I had helped alter. But maybe someday, someone would find the key, and the past as we'd always known it would at last be wiped clean of bloodshed.

These were the thoughts that floated through my head as I walked onstage to accept my diploma, my parents smiling proudly from the audience. I had done what I had always intended to do with my life; I'd accomplished my goal. But now, what to do next? I wasn't at all sure I wanted to be a historian anymore; I knew too much now to believe in it as a rational field of study. And I couldn't imagine lecturing a class of freshman students about World War II without being able to share my own experience with them, to make history truly resonate with them in a way few people left alive would be able to do. And if I couldn't do that, what was the point of teaching at all? I didn't know. I needed time to think, to figure out my next step.

And that's when Mom came through for me, as she always has.

―――――――――――

London, England
June 2010

When on the verge of a post-graduate existential crisis, take a vacation. At least, that seemed like a good solution to me, and my mom agreed.

After my commencement ceremony, she and my dad hugged me, congratulated me on my shiny new doctorate, and offered their graduation gift: a trip anywhere in the world. I'd worked so hard these past eight years, they said; they wanted to give me a break for some rest and relaxation. I accepted gratefully.

I probably should have taken them up on a trip to Tahiti, or Brazil, or the Maldives: some far-flung, sunny location I'd never likely make it to on my own. But the truth was, there was only one place in the world I really felt called back to at that point in my life. Luckily, when I told Mom what I wanted, she was on board with my idea. So, in late June, we headed back to London together.

We had a lovely two weeks in England. Most of it was spent with family, our close-knit clan that had been created, I now realized, through Molly's sacrifice, or at least through her life's twists and turns.

And on the last day, we visited Molly herself.

———————————

I had never been to my grandmother's grave. I didn't go to her funeral. I was twenty-three when she died, at the impressive age of eight-eight, and I had just begun graduate school. I was swamped with papers to write and books to read, and, in any case, I had no money for the plane ticket. I did ask my mom if she wanted me to go with her, and if she'd said yes, I would have found a way to make the trip work. But she didn't insist I accompany her; she told me to stay home, focus on my studies, and not to worry about missing the funeral. I have to admit I was relieved.

Looking back on all this years later, I was astounded by my selfishness, my indifference to the woman who had given life to the woman who'd given me life. Even if I hadn't ultimately met Molly and become her friend, I like to think I would still have been able to see from the perch of a few years of maturity how wrong I'd been to basically shrug at my grandmother's death. True, I had never really known her, as her granddaughter. We hardly ever visited her, and she'd refused to fly all the way to America to see us. My childhood memories of her were all but nonexistent—but still. She was my grandmother, my mother's mother. That should have been enough to motivate me to get on a plane to say goodbye to her, whatever minor effort of time and money it might have cost me.

I felt I would never be able to repay the debts I was accruing to Molly. Taking stock of my life, of who I'd been in relation to the people I loved and owed the most to, did not produce a comforting picture. I was a good daughter, but a mediocre granddaughter, and a horrible friend.

I knew it was too late to make any of that up to Molly. But perhaps it was never too late to apologize.

———————————

Mom and I stood silently side by side, staring at the tombstone. It was only the second time she'd been here—the only time aside from the funeral—and she'd brought some flowers to put on the grave. And I imagine she'd also brought a certain degree of guilt, for not coming here until I suggested it. *That's so sweet of you to want to visit your grandmother in the cemetery*, she'd said when I suggested it during the planning of our trip. My own guilt only multiplied under the weight of her innocent praise.

I don't know what my mom was thinking as she stared down at the place that held the last earthly remains of the woman who'd brought her into the world. I didn't ask. We all have our share of guilt, I realized by now, and my mom's was her own to work through, unless she chose to share it. I didn't want to pry.

Eventually, Mom seemed to grow weary of standing in silence at Molly's grave, and she told me she would take a walk to see the other members of her family who were buried nearby. My grandfather Patrick and my mom's younger brother, who'd died a few years ago, were laid to rest here as well. She walked off and left me alone, standing over Molly's casket, a smattering of useless flowers in my hands.

Once my mother was out of earshot, I began to talk. I'm not a terribly spiritual person, and I don't claim to know what happens to a person after they die, but I had a deep conviction that Molly could hear me. I remembered what my mom used to say about her when I was a child: *My mother had eyes in the back of her head. Ears too. She always knew when you were up to something.*

All I wanted now was for her to hear me. I wasn't sure if I was after forgiveness, or atonement, or just acknowledgment of my own regrets. But I knew I had to speak.

"Hi, Molly. I guess you're pretty surprised to see me, huh? Or maybe not. Maybe now, wherever you are, you know the truth about everything that happened all those years ago—who I really was, what I was doing there when you and I crossed paths in London by chance that day in the pub. Isn't that amazing? Of all the people I could have met . . ." My voice trailed off, and I wasn't sure how to continue.

"Anyway, I didn't come here today to talk about me. I wanted to visit you, and let you know I'll always remember you, and not just the you I knew when you were older, once you'd become my grandmother." I shook my head. In my mind, I saw Molly working at the pub, scrubbing bedpans in the hospital, coming to my flat to tell me she had ended things with Patrick, and then a few months later, making her return visit to give me the news that my mom was on her way. She'd been so young, so pretty . . . It was hard to attach the term *grandmother* to that young girl with dark hair and rosy cheeks and pale Irish skin and feel like it meant anything. Two different people altogether, one falling into the other as she grew older, sadder, probably wiser. Yet the connection between those young and old women was real and impossible to ignore; it was standing a hundred feet from me now, putting flowers on her father's grave.

"If you know everything now, I guess you know why I wanted you and Patrick to be together. I tried to make it sound like I wasn't interfering in your choice, after the accident at the factory—but the truth was, I knew I was going to have to push you back together, one way or another. That was just the opening I'd been waiting for. I knew—I realized that you were happy living without him, training to be a nurse, a career woman. I saw that. You used to have this glow in your eyes when you talked about the work we were doing. I could see how much you loved it, how much it meant to you. If I'd only seen the beginning of your story—if I could have just been your friend, your contemporary—I would have wanted that life for you more than anything.

"But that's not how it was, as you must know by now. The truth is, there may have been more than one you—the young nurse, the devoted mother, the gray-haired, slow-walking grandmother I remember from the last time we visited you here—but there was only ever one Vivienne. The girl who was your friend, who your granddaughter was named after—she was me all along. We were caught in an endless loop, a circle with no beginning and no end. There was no way I could stand back and let you alter your life without erasing mine—and Mom's, and your other children and grandchildren. So, I sacrificed you for us."

My eyes teared up as I spoke these words.

"And the thing is this—everything I am is because of you. If I hadn't been born, raised in the time and place I was, able to get a good education and live the life I wanted to live, I never would have been chosen to come back in the first place. I never would have met you. And really, I may be giving myself too much credit, too much power in your story. Maybe I didn't change anything about your life after all—maybe it was all predestined, meant to be. Maybe the real reason I needed to go back was to meet you, to know who you were back then so I would understand how much you gave up for the rest of us. So I'd appreciate the life you've given me, and never forget."

Through my tears, I began to smile, and for the first time since Andrew's death, I felt something—not happiness, exactly, but peace. Maybe I hadn't been the one to take away Molly's choices, to alter the course of her life after all. Maybe she would ultimately have made the same decisions and lived the same life regardless of whether we'd met when she was a young woman. But we did meet, and we touched one another's lives in a way we never could have done in linear fashion. All those years later, Molly had never forgotten me—that was the reason I had my name. And I would never forget her. And if I someday was lucky enough to have a daughter, I'd make sure she knew the story of the extraordinary woman who had been her great-grandmother—and long before that, in another time and place, her mother's friend.

If my debt to Molly could never be repaid exactly, I now felt like it had been cancelled out, forgiven by a generous lender. I laid the flowers down on the mound of earth that covered Molly's bones, took one last look at her headstone, and walked away.

The End

ABOUT THE AUTHOR

Melissa Kaplan was born in Connecticut and has lived for most of her life in the Washington, DC, region, where she works as an advocate on food security and hunger policy. She studied at the London School of Economics and Political Science, earning a master's degree in comparative politics with a focus on Europe. She has been a passionate student of history her entire life, particularly the World War II era, which helped inspire her to write this book.

Melissa is an avid traveler who has lived in London and Prague and visited over forty countries. In addition to traveling and writing, Melissa enjoys yoga, barre, and kickboxing classes, as well as reading, working on political campaigns, and planning future travels. She is currently at work on her second novel.

ABOUT BOLD STORY PRESS

Bold Story Press is a curated, woman-owned hybrid publishing company with a mission of publishing well-written stories by women. If your book is chosen for publication, our team of expert editors and designers will work with you to publish a professionally edited and designed book. Every woman has a story to tell. If you have written yours and want to explore publishing with Bold Story Press, contact us at https://boldstorypress.com.

**BOLD
STORY
PRESS**

The Bold Story Press logo, designed by Grace Arsenault, was inspired by the nom de plume, or pen name, a sad necessity at one time for female authors who wanted to publish. The woman's face hidden in the quill is the profile of Virginia Woolf, who, in addition to being an early feminist writer, founded and ran her own publishing company, Hogarth Press.

CPSIA information can be obtained
at www.ICGtesting.com
Printed in the USA
BVHW042000090523
663856BV00005B/7